"Not everything may be as it seems"

GOBLIN HALL

A FANTASY ADVENTURE

peter kerr

Oasis-WERP

Published by Oasis-WERP 2020

ISBN: 978-0-9576586-9-1

www.peter-kerr.co.uk

Cover design © Glen Kerr

Typeset by Glen Kerr

(Chapter heading image courtesy
Goblin Ha' Hotel, Gifford, Scotland)

ABOUT THE AUTHOR

Best-selling Scottish author Peter Kerr is a former jazz
musician, record producer and farmer. His award-winning
Snowball Oranges series of humorous travelogues was inspired
by his family's adventures while running a small orange
farm on the Spanish island of Mallorca during the 1980s.
Peter's books, written with warmth, gutsy style and spiky
humour, are sold worldwide and have been translated into
several languages. He is married, with two grown-up sons,
and lives in East Lothian.

www.peter-kerr.co.uk

TABLE OF CONTENTS

– CHAPTER ONE –

THE PRESENT DAY –
A SCOTTISH COUNTRY VILLAGE...

Maggie McKim's heart was heavy. Just turned thirty, she had been left to care for her two children alone, following the recent death of her husband Jim. Moving into a little cottage after living in the rambling old manse which had gone with Jim's position as parish minister didn't bother her, but the thought of bringing up two young children without him certainly did. At only seven and five respectively, little Susie and Jamie were at an age when a father's influence and support were needed most, but now it was up to Maggie to cope as best she could on her own. The prospect frightened her, she had to admit, but for the children's sake she had no choice but to put on a brave face and try to make life seem as normal as possible.

She signed the removal man's list, thanked him and turned to go indoors. Charlie, the family's tiny mongrel dog, came running round the side of the cottage, tongue hanging out, tail wagging, eyes sparkling, full of the joys.

Maggie bent down to tickle his chin. 'Well, Charlie, been exploring your new garden, have you? Plenty nice new smells to sniff, are there?'

Charlie yelped a 'You bet!' little bark, then trotted over to the side of the front door, lifted his leg and shot a squirt or two of territory-marking pee on the old iron boot scraper.

Maggie chuckled and shook her head. If only life could be as simple and carefree for her as it appeared to be for Charlie. She paused to look at her new home – the first chance she'd had to grab a moment's respite in days. Moving house was indeed an exhausting business, and there was lots of work still to do. For all that, she gladly admitted there were worse places to have moved to than Cantrip Cottage, sitting as it did on the edge of the pretty village of Burnford, with a little valley called Trowie Glen at the back, and beyond that the wooded hills of the Scottish countryside.

It was all very tranquil and picturesque, and Maggie smiled as she told herself that she and the children would be fine here. Life without Jim wasn't going to be easy, but she realised that she was luckier than many in her shoes. At least she had a little place she'd soon make into a comfortable home. Yes, she, Susie and Jamie would be fine. Holding that positive thought, Maggie opened the door for the patiently-waiting Charlie and followed him inside.

Old Effie had been Maggie's housekeeper back at the manse, and as she lived at this side of the village herself, she'd insisted on helping her move into the cottage. When Maggie entered the living room, Effie was already fussing about with the three-piece suite, placing an easy chair here, rolling the sofa there, standing back to have a look, tutting, then rearranging everything again.

'Don't go bothering yourself with that,' said Maggie. 'Honestly, Effie, you've done more than enough for one day.'

'Och, but you can't do all this by yourself, Mrs McKim.' Effie nodded towards the piles of cardboard boxes the removal men had dumped on the floor. 'I mean, just look at it!'

Maggie laid a hand on Effie's shoulder. 'Come on, sit down and take the weight off your feet. I'll make us a nice cuppa. I think we deserve it, hmm?'

'No, no, no,' Effie objected, 'you've more to worry about than me and my feet, Mrs McKim.' But she sat down on the sofa all the same.

Maggie was already at the kitchen door. 'Just you relax,' she called back. 'Oh, and it's Maggie, by the way. I think we can forget about all that formal Mrs McKim stuff now, don't you?'

Effie surveyed the topsy-turvy state of the room, her brows gathering into a frown. 'What would the poor Reverend say if he could see what's become of his bonny wife and nice wee bairns now?' she muttered to herself, her bottom lip quivering. 'Aye, and him that young too.' The old woman looked over to where Susie and Jamie were poring over a picture book at a table in front of the window. 'The poor wee mites,' she sniffed, and dabbed her eyes with her hankie. 'The poor wee mites.'

'The usual two sugars?' Maggie shouted from the kitchen.

'Oh, uh-huh, please, Mrs ehm...' Effie warbled, unable to disguise the sadness in her voice.

'Stop it, Charlie!' Susie scolded, after the little dog had leapt onto a chair next to her and tried to nose his way into the company of his two young playmates. 'Me and Jamie are busy!' With that, she continued to explain in hushed tones to her little brother some fascinating detail or other in their book.

Maggie came back into the room carrying a tea tray. 'It's "Jamie and I", Susie,' she pointed out, 'not "me and Jamie". I keep telling you that, don't I?'

Susie didn't even look up. 'Yes, yes, OK, Mum,' she mumbled, clearly not having taken in a word her mother had said.

'Anything to drink for you two?' Maggie enquired. 'Milk, Jamie? Orange juice or something, Susie?'

'No thanks, Mum,' the children replied in unison, their eyes fixed firmly on the book lying open in front of them.

Effie took a sip of her tea, then cast her eyes sadly round the room. 'This wee place – I mean, what a change this must be for you, Mrs McKim – after living in that grand big manse and everything.'

'Not a bit of it,' Maggie chirped. 'No, no, I was brought up in a house even smaller than this, and it'll suit our purpose just fine, believe me. To tell you the truth, I'm only too pleased the church offered to rent it to me, otherwise we'd...' She stopped short, something through the window having caught her eye. 'What – who on *earth* is that?'

Effie stood up and shuffled over to the window, half-closing her eyes, trying to focus.

Susie and Jamie followed the old housekeeper's gaze, nudging each other as they noticed the figure of an old man, standing alone beneath a dead tree on top of a grassy little hill some distance behind the house. His long, wispy hair and flowing robe were blowing in the breeze. He was looking skywards, his hands outstretched, as if offering up some sort of prayer.

'Ach, it's just Mr Mungo,' Effie finally grunted. 'Always doing that. Fair gives you the willies, so it does!'

Maggie had joined Effie by the window. 'But – but what in heaven's name is he doing – you know, just standing there like that, looking at … nothing?'

Effie merely shrugged, her expression a mix of indifference and distrust.

Puzzled, Maggie shook her head. 'Mr Mungo, you say. But I've never heard of … I mean, I thought I knew *every*one in the village.'

'Only arrived a week or so back,' Effie said. 'From nowhere. Moved into that wee cottage down the bottom of the glen there.' She pointed through the window. 'Granny Carlin's place. Aye, he moved in just after she passed away.' Effie cupped a hand to her mouth, then, hoping the children wouldn't hear, whispered in Maggie's ear, 'Granny Carlin … her they called a witch.'

Maggie gave a little smile, though a frown creased her forehead for a second. She hoped they weren't going to be living close to some old weirdo with habits that might scare the children. That's *all* she needed!

Susie and Jamie exchanged knowing glances. Then, while their mother and Effie returned to the sofa with their cups of tea, they redirected their eyes to their book. It was open at a drawing of an old man, who was dressed and looked exactly like the one they could see through the window. More fascinating still, the picture also showed him standing in a similar pose beneath the branches of a dead tree on top of a windswept hill.

Susie ran her finger slowly along the caption beneath the picture. *'The Wizard Of The Glen'*, she told her little brother in a whisper.

Unaware of the children's discovery, Effie jerked her head in the direction of the window. 'Aye – Mr Mungo, your new neighbour,' she muttered to Maggie out of the corner of her mouth, then shuddered, her teacup rattling on its saucer. 'Fair gives me the heebie-jeebies, so he does!'

* * * * *

– CHAPTER TWO –

LATER THAT MORNING –
AT THE FOOT OF TROWIE GLEN...

Granny Carlin's cottage was said to be the oldest lived-in house in the area. Its roof had been clad in red pantiles for as long as anyone could remember, although the tiny building probably dated from times when thatch, or perhaps even turf, was used instead. The cottage didn't boast much in the way of modern conveniences. It had no electricity or gas, no telephone or TV, and the only source of water was an ancient hand-operated pump, of the type reproduced in fibreglass these days to stand alongside plastic gnomes and fake wishing wells in trim suburban gardens.

But this simple little abode was sufficient for old Mungo's needs. He knew well enough that Granny Carlin had been regarded as a witch by some of the village folk, and that was fine by his way of thinking. Just why they had doubted her supernatural powers was the only thing that puzzled him. Anyway, he was happy to be living in the cottage now. He had known the location intimately many, many years ago, and he loved it dearly – no matter how time had changed everything, and not really for the better, in his opinion. However, sitting on his rickety rocking chair by the front door, as he was now, and looking over the burn towards the woods on the other side of the glen, he could still be living in his glory days of long ago ... *if* he gave free rein to his imagination.

'*Al-ga-boo-ra-ba zi-ba-no*, Jake,' he enunciated patiently to the young jackdaw sitting on his hand, its head cocked inquisitively to one side, its pale blue eyes gleaming like tiny glass marbles. 'Repeat after me, Jake ... *Al-ga-boo-ra-ba zi-ba-no*.'

The jackdaw said nothing.

Mungo sighed and got to his feet.

'You a wizard?'

Startled, Jake flew off, while Mungo glanced down in the direction of the question. Susie and Jamie were standing there looking up at him, with Charlie the dog by their side.

'You a wizard?' Susie repeated.

Mungo peered at the children over the top of the half-moon spectacles that were perched on the end of his nose, giving him the appearance of an amiable, if somewhat skinny, old owl. 'Hello,' he smiled. 'Where did you appear fro–?'

'Why were you saying funny words to that crow?' Susie cut in.

'You mean Jake? Well, uhm, Jake's a jackdaw actually. Hmm.'

Susie stared thoughtfully at Mungo for a moment. 'Our book says wizards can talk to jackdaws.'

'*My* book,' Jamie corrected. '*Wizard of the Hen*'.

Scowling, Susie nudged her little brother with her elbow. 'Glen, silly. It's *Wizard of the* Glen.'

'And does your book also say that jackdaws can talk to wizards?' Mungo asked.

'Yes,' Susie and Jamie confirmed in concert.

The old man hunched his shoulders. 'Well, 'fraid my one can't. Stupid bird.'

'Get a budgie,' Jamie advised. 'Our granny's got a budgie and it can talk.'

'Wizards don't have budgies, silly,' Susie said under her breath.

Jamie gave that some thought, then looked up at Mungo again. 'You a wizard, mister?' he pressed.

'Well, uhm, yes ... yes, as a matter of fact I am,' Mungo said, surprising himself by having seemed a bit reluctant to admit it. 'A wizard? Yes, I am, uhm ... actually. Yes.'

'Can you do magic?' Jamie enquired, hopefully.

Mungo chuckled to himself. He was enjoying the interest the children were taking in him. 'Magic? Yes, I – I can. But I'm, well, I'm sort of semi-retired these days, you see.' He scratched his head. 'But, uh, let's see now.' He beckoned Jamie to step nearer, then reached down and produced a copper coin from the little boy's nose. 'There! What do you think of *that*?'

Susie was clearly unimpressed. 'That's not real magic,' she scoffed. 'Our Daddy could do that. Yes, and he's only a minister.'

'Well, you know – magic, miracles, all much the same really,' Mungo blustered, feeling embarrassed. 'When, uh, when you come to think of it, that is.'

Jamie stared at him, expressionless. 'Our Daddy's in heaven now.'

The old fellow's eyes misted over. 'Oh, my... Sorry, I –'

'Why be sorry?' Susie interrupted. 'Heaven's a nice place.'

'Yes,' Jamie agreed, 'and our Mummy says we're all going to see Daddy there some day.'

Mungo smiled kindly at Jamie and ruffled his hair. 'And so you will ... if you believe. Everything is possible, if you really believe, you know.'

Jamie looked down at his feet, muttering: 'I really believe I'd like to see Daddy, *now*.'

A moment of awkward silence followed, broken by Jake the jackdaw fluttering down onto the guttering above the cottage door. '*Boorabba*!' he confidently squawked. '*Algaboorabba*!'

Mungo was flabbergasted. He stood gazing wide-eyed at Jake. 'At last!' he grinned. 'He's finally –'

'*Algaboorabba*!' Jake repeated.

Susie and Jamie burst into fits of giggles.

Charlie the dog let out a nervous little growl and took a couple of cautious steps backwards.

'*Alga*-thingy,' Susie said to Mungo, '– is that a magic word?'

'Well... yes. But, uhm, you have to add –'

'*Zibanno*,' Jake butted in. '*Algaboorabba zibanno*!'

There was a minor thunder clap and a flash of lightning, a momentary rush of howling wind, then a bright gold coin dropped from Jamie's nose and landed at his feet. Charlie whimpered and cowered behind Susie's legs. Staring at the coin, the children gasped in amazement. After a moment or two, Jamie hesitantly touched his nose, as if afraid it might burn his finger.

Old Mungo couldn't hide his delight at Jake's sudden and unexpected show, not just of speaking, but of magical ability too. The old man bent down and picked up the glittering coin. 'Well, well, well,' he beamed, 'would you believe it?'

Jake, thoroughly pleased with himself, gave a cackling laugh, then triumphantly cawed, '*Algaboorabba Zibanno*!'

Up at her cottage, meanwhile, Maggie was busy cleaning windows. She couldn't actually see Mungo and the children from where she was, but she could hear the thunder and see the flashes of lightning coming from somewhere at the foot of the glen. 'There it goes again,' she said to herself. 'What on *earth*...?

Back at Mungo's cottage, Susie squealed in delight as a gold coin dropped from her nose this time.

Smiling to himself, Mungo picked up the coin. 'Would you believe it?' he said again, then looked up to where Jake was perched above the cottage door. 'Clever boy! Here, Jake – come and see.'

Jake swooped down and landed on Mungo's shoulder, whereupon the old man produced a titbit from a pocket in his robe and popped it into the eager young jackdaw's beak.

'*Stupid bird*!' squawked Jake, showing off now. '*Silly bugger*!'

A shocked, sharp intake of breath was the children's immediate reaction to Jake's unexpected but fluently-delivered swear word. Mungo was abashed to the point of being dumbstruck. But his embarrassment was relieved slightly by Susie and Jamie dissolving into fits of tittering.

'Oh, my, m-my,' Mungo stammered, 'I really am very –'

'Bugger!' said Jamie, straight-faced, then joined Susie in another outburst of giggling.

Smitten by the children's infectious sense of mischief, Mungo smiled, tentatively at first, then grinned, before joining in the laughter himself, his eyes twinkling like little black pearls as he handed Susie and Jamie their gold coins.

'Well, really,' he panted, wiping his eyes while struggling to regain his composure, 'I really don't know where he heard such language. No, I really don't.'

Almost as if in response to his master's somewhat lame protestation, Jake let out a volley of croaky chuckles, plopped a large dropping onto Mungo's shoulder, then flew away. Susie and Jamie covered their mouths with their hands, trying hard not to start sniggering again.

Mungo gave them an enquiring look, then glanced round at his shoulder. 'Oh, no!' he groaned. 'If I've told that bird once that it isn't polite to do that, I've told him a hundred times.'

By this time, the children were purple in the face with bottled up glee. Mungo looked at them again and, despite himself, felt a giggle building up inside as well. A moment later, all three were engulfed in yet more floods of laughter.

Susie was laughing so much she almost choked. 'That's – that's 'cause you told a fib about not knowing how the bird knows that bad word,' she spluttered, pointing at the jackdaw dump dribbling down Mungo's robe.

Just then, a call of '*Susie*! *Jamie*!' rang out across the valley, and the children turned round to see their mother stepping purposefully down the grassy slope from her cottage. 'I thought I told you two not to wander off!'

'Mummy,' Jamie piped up, keen to be first to divulge the reason for the present outbreak of hilarity, 'this old man's got a blackbird and –'

Stopping Jamie short in mid sentence, Maggie extended her hand to Mungo. 'Hello there. You must be Mr Mungo,' she smiled. 'I'm Maggie – Maggie McKim – from Cantrip Cottage, up the glen there.'

'Ah, enchanted to meet you, dear lady,' Mungo smiled back. He bowed courteously and shook Maggie's hand.

Jamie could hardly contain himself. 'But, Mummy,' he persisted, 'the blackbird said bu–'

'Sh-h-h, Jamie! I'm talking, and you know it's rude to interrupt.' Maggie turned again to Mungo. 'I hope Susie and Jamie haven't been annoying you.'

'No, no, Mistress McKim – on the contrary. No, I haven't laughed so much for ages.' He scratched his head again. 'Well, not for a century or two anyway.'

Maggie smiled, weakly. 'Hmm, yes … quite.'

Susie tapped her mother's elbow. 'Mummy, Jamie

said bu–'

Mungo faked a cough. 'A-*hum*! And, uh, it's just Mungo, dear lady. No Mister.'

Maggie was taken aback. 'Oh dear, I'm really sorry. Really, I didn't realise it was your first name. Please forgive me. I didn't mean to be forward, honestly, Mr, uhm...?'

'Mungo.'

'Mungo? But, ehm...' Maggie was becoming more confused by the second.

Mungo shrugged. 'Just Mungo. I only have the one name, you see. We, uh, we *all* do.'

'We?'

'He's a wizard,' Susie offered by way of explanation.

'And his blackbird said bugger,' Jamie announced, grabbing the opportunity to get a word in edgeways at last.

Maggie glared at her little son, who, radiating innocence, returned her glare with a grin.

Susie sniggered behind her hand.

'He, uhm, Jake – he's a jackdaw, actually,' Mungo flustered. He flashed Maggie a sheepish smile. 'Not a blackbird – a jackdaw – a young one. Just learning to speak.' Mungo cleared his throat. 'Yes, well, he – he probably meant to say beggar ... or, you know, burglar. All the same to a rookie jackdaw, I suppose.'

The arching of an unconvinced eyebrow was Maggie's response to that one.

An uncomfortable little lull in the conversation followed, during which Jamie put a thumb to one of his nostrils and snorted loudly down the other.

'Jamie!' Maggie exclaimed. 'That's absolutely

disgusting!'

'He's trying to magic out some more money,' Susie explained

Maggie shook her head despairingly. 'Their father – he – well, he used to do that old sleight of hand trick for them,' she told Mungo. 'You know the one – pennies popping out of their noses.'

Mungo gave her an understanding smile.

Jamie, meanwhile, was applying a thumb to his other nostril, concentrating hard. '*Boola-boola-boola*,' he droned, then blasted another nasal snort. Another unsuccessful one.

'*Boola-boola*'s not the magic word, silly,' Susie scoffed.

Jamie scowled and stuck a finger up his nose, totally bamboozled.

Maggie was trying to smile through her embarrassment. 'Look, sorry about all this,' she said to Mungo. 'They're reading a book about a wizard just now, you see. And, well, you know how it is – every elderly gentleman they see at the moment is a wizard, every big new word a magic spell.'

Mungo nodded, knowingly. 'They believe.'

'Yes, I'm afraid they do. Just at that gullible age. Still, only fairy stories – won't do them any harm, I suppose.'

A self-assured look came to Mungo's face. 'Believe in the good, deny the bad.' He shook his head. 'Not gullible, Mistress McKim. Wise. Your children are at that *wise* age.' He wagged a finger at Maggie. 'Don't spoil them. Let them believe.'

This was all beginning to make Maggie feel distinctly uncomfortable. She couldn't say she was getting any really *bad* vibes from this dotty old guy, but she didn't need a lecture from him on how to bring up her kids either. Besides, what was all this dressing-up-in-long-robes thing about? Time to put out a feeler or two...

'Ehm, I hope you don't mind my asking, Mister, uhm, Mungo, but where are you from? I mean, before you came to live here, that is.'

Mungo's eyes twinkled and he gave a little chuckle. 'Me? Oh, everywhere, really – at some time or other.' He paused to stroke his chin for a moment. 'Mind you, now that I think about it, I haven't been to Outer Mongolia for a while. Hmm, couldn't get on with that terrible fellow Khan. Yes ... what did they call him again?'

Maggie squinted at him. 'Not – not *Genghis*, by any –?'

'Yes! That's him! Genghis Khan ... the very one!' Mungo became pensive again. 'Mmm, Genghis Khan. He suffered from constipation, you know. And no wonder – eating all those sheep's eyeballs. A unique outlook on life, some said his diet gave him. Hmm, nasty fellow, all the same.'

Maggie scrutinised Mungo's face, looking for a sign that he might be joking. But it seemed the old boy was being deadly serious. 'You – you're saying you actually *knew*...?'

'Genghis Khan? Oh yes. Didn't like him at all. Bad table manners too. Flatulence, you know. Hmm, the big wind from the Steppes, some used to call him.'

'But he lived over eight hundred years ago, for heaven's sake!'

'Yes, doesn't time fly,' Mungo nodded, then added with a wink, 'when you're having fun, as they say.'

That did it for Maggie. She took Susie and Jamie by the shoulders. 'Come on! Time to go home! Time to let Mister – to let *Mungo* here get on with his –'

'No hurry,' Mungo interrupted, a smile on his lips that would have warmed the iciest of hearts. He gestured towards his cottage door. 'Come inside. Have a cup of tea. Yes, tea. I, uh, I picked some fresh nettles this morning. Or if you prefer,' he continued, noticing Maggie's less than keen reaction, 'I have some nice dried dandelion leaves. They make a tasty brew. Ah! Very good for the digestion too, dandelion leaves … as you probably know.' He winked again. 'If only Genghis Khan had known as well, eh?'

Maggie was already shepherding the children away. 'No – no thank you, all the same. Perhaps … well, maybe some other –'

'*Yoo-hoo! Yoo-hoo-oo-oo*!' It was old Effie's shrill voice, reverberating down the glen from outside the back door of Maggie's cottage. 'Phone call for you Mrs McKim!'

Flustered, Maggie spoke to the children first. 'Look, I'll have to rush. But you two follow *right* after me. Understand?'

'Ye-e-e-s, Mum,' they droned.

'*Telephone*!' Effie yelled, but with some urgency now.

'Sorry, Mr, ehm…' Maggie called over her

shoulder as she set off up the hillside. 'As I say, perhaps some other…'

Mungo gave her a wave and a smile. 'Don't you go worrying, mistress. We'll have that cup of brew another time, sure enough.'

Susy and Jamie, who had scarcely taken their eyes off Mungo, were clearly now more interested in resuming their dialogue with him than obeying their mother's order to head straight home.

'Our book says wizards can make things fly,' Susie stated for openers.

'Very true,' Mungo affirmed, pursing his lips and nodding. 'Very true.'

'So?' Susie prompted.

Mungo raised a wary eyebrow, but said nothing.

'So, can *you*?'

'M-make things fly?'

'That's right.'

Mungo shrugged, trying to appear more sure of himself than he actually felt. 'Why, yes. Well, I used to. But, as I say, I – I'm sort of retired now.' He rolled his shoulders. 'You know, sort of … resting.'

'Mummy makes me rest when I'm tired too,' Jamie confessed with a sigh.

Susie tutted and glared at her little brother in the way big sisters do. '*Re*-tired, silly! That's different from just tired. *Re*-tired only affects very old people.'

Old Mungo didn't seem to have heard this little exchange. He was gazing up the glen, deep in thought. 'It's the Power,' he said, as if to himself. 'Yes, I've let the Power slip a bit of late, I'm afraid.'

Susie and Jamie followed the old man's gaze to

the hill where they'd seen him standing under a dead tree earlier in the day.

'Hmm, the Power,' Mungo murmured trance-like, while a peal of thunder rumbled in the distance.

Susie was intrigued, but Jamie's mind was on something else. 'Can you make Jasper fly?' he asked Mungo.

This jolted the old man out of his musing. '*Oh!*' he gasped, clearly surprised to see a white mouse hanging by its tail from the little boy's fingers.

'Well, *can* you?' Jamie urged.

Mungo grinned self-confidently. 'Make a mouse fly? Easy!' But the smile then faded from his face. He shuffled his feet. 'Well, uhm, it *used* to be easy, but as I say – since I sort of retired...'

Susie wasn't slow to stick the verbal boot in. 'You can't do it, can you?'

'Yes, I – I mean, no,' Mungo stammered. 'Well, yes, but it's just that...' Stuck for words, he lowered his eyes.

Jamie frowned, clearly disillusioned, then stuffed Jasper the mouse back into his pocket.

Susie took her little brother by the arm, preparing to leave, but hesitated, struck by a sudden thought. 'Oh, and give me your penny, Jamie,' she said.

Jamie duly gave her the gold coin which Jake the jackdaw had magicked from his nose.

Susie then handed Mungo Jamie's gold coin, and her own. 'Here,' she snapped, somehow managing to look up at Mungo while looking down her nose at the same time, 'you can work your silly conjuring tricks on somebody else!' With that, she told Jamie in a stage whisper that Mungo wasn't a real wizard. The two children then trudged contemptuously off, with Charlie the dog trotting faithfully behind.

Crestfallen, Mungo watched them go, his thoughts in turmoil. 'No! Wait!' he called after a moment. 'Come back ... please!'

The children stopped and turned to face him, their expressions daring him not to disappoint them again.

As a counter measure, Mungo immediately adopted a self-assured attitude – or at least did his best to fake one. 'I can, I *will* do it!' he told himself, then motioned to Jamie. 'The mouse. Give me – I mean, h-hand me the mouse ... please.'

Jamie wasn't sure. 'You'll make him fly?' he asked, warily.

'Of course! Why not? I've done it hundreds of times. Thousands. Millions. I mean, where do you think bats came from?'

All Jamie knew about bats was that he didn't like them. Old Effie said that, if they got tangled in your hair, you had to have it all cut off to get them out. So, he wasn't interested in where bats came from, just so long as they didn't come near *him*. Still, what old Mungo had claimed sounded fairly convincing. Jamie pulled the white mouse from his pocket and handed it over, albeit a little reluctantly. 'Don't be fright'ed, Jasper,' he murmured while stroking the little creature's head. 'I'm here.'

If Jasper cared one way or the other, he certainly didn't show it, sniffing about short-sightedly on the palm of Mungo's hand, whiskers twitching. The prospect of a nice morsel of cheese or chocolate may well have been on his mind – although, unlike his young owner, concerns about whether or not he was about to become airborne were, presumably, farthest from his thoughts.

Mungo, meanwhile, was well aware that this was make-or-break time: perhaps his one and only chance to prove to the children that he was indeed a genuine wizard, and not just a long-haired old oddball who made boasts he couldn't live up to. Calming himself, he cradled Jasper in his hands, closed his eyes, took a slow, deep breath, then pulled himself up to his full height, his head tilted backwards.

Susie and Jamie looked on, enthralled, impatient for the real magic stuff to start.

'*O-o-oh-h-h, baglan-nalgab*,' Mungo moaned, his voice trembling. '*Baglanagab-hum-m-m.*'

Jasper, still wingless, continued to sniff about on the palms of the old man's hands, blissfully unaware of the unfolding drama in which he was sharing a starring role. Susie and Jamie swapped doubting glances.

Strange, guttural noises began to gurgle in Mungo's throat. Then he started to quiver, very slightly at first, the movements gradually becoming more pronounced, until his whole body was shaking like a jelly. Suddenly, he opened his eyes wide.

'*Baglanagab zibanno!*' he yelled, leaping up and throwing Jasper into the air with a frantic shout of, '*FLY!*'

Fascinated, Susie and Jamie watched the mouse spin upwards to a height of a metre or so, only to be drawn back down by the force of gravity into Mungo's trembling hands. He smiled sheepishly at the children, who glowered back, conspicuously unimpressed. 'Uhm-ah, lack of practice,' he said with an embarrassed little laugh. 'Lack of the Power, you know. Still, second time lucky, eh?'

After clearing his throat, Mungo started his warm-up routine all over again, though taking not one, but several deep breaths this time. The gurgling noises and trembling started as before, but even louder and more violent now. Startled by this grotesque ritual, the children clung to each other as Mungo began another spell...

'O-o-oh-h-h, baglan-baglan,' he moaned, his voice rising. 'Baglanagab ooblan moosus!' Then, with a sudden leap, he threw Jasper as high as he could, yelling, 'Zibanno-o-o! Baglanagab zibanno-o-o! FLY, OH MOUSE!'

Mungo and the children looked up open-mouthed at the somersaulting Jasper reaching a height of four metres, where he hovered for a tantalising moment before starting to drop earthwards again. Then, just as Susie was about to voice her dissatisfaction in no uncertain terms, there was a loud 'POP!', and the mouse was engulfed in an explosion of dazzling light, suspended in mid air like a miniature distress flare.

The children caught their breaths. Charlie growled nervously behind their legs, while a smile of relieved optimism began to spread over Mungo's face. He continued to stare upwards, his eyes on sticks.

'Spread your wings, oh tiny one!' he implored.

But no sooner had the halo of light around Jasper started to dissolve than it became apparent that, instead of sprouting wings, he was self-inflating, expanding in circumference until he became a football-size mouse-balloon, drifting in the breeze and squeaking in bewilderment.

'Oops!' muttered Mungo, mortified.

'Jasper!' whispered Jamie, distraught.

'*That's* not really flying!' Susie declared as she scowled her disapproval.

'Try telling that to the mouse,' the old man mumbled, his expression a strange mix of satisfaction and worry, while he watched the victim of his bungled magic floating up, up and away.

Then, with another '*POP!*', followed by a sort of high-pitched farting sound, Jasper began to deflate, zig-zagging at speed towards his launch pad, Mungo's outstretched hands.

Susie and Jamie clung to each other again, almost afraid to look at their pet spiralling out of control. Grimacing, Mungo closed his eyes, waiting for the impact. Yet, inexplicably, with only a few feet to go, Jasper's nosedive suddenly halted and he was transformed into a shimmering vapour within a luminous cloud, from which a howling wind began to blow, whipping up dust and leaves from the ground below.

Mungo pulled the children to him. He wrapped his robe about them with one hand, while shielding his eyes from the blinding glare of the cloud with the other. Charlie the dog quickly got the message and scampered off whimpering behind the cottage, his tail firmly between his legs.

Suddenly, the sound of manic laughter echoed

through the glen, and within the ghostly cloud there materialised the face of a man, his long hair billowing wildly, his satanic green eyes more menacing than a snake's, his mouth contorted into an evil grin. He threw his head back and laughed again.

Mungo gaped at this awful apparition. 'Zorn!' he gulped, his voice thick with foreboding.

Susie and Jamie peeked out trembling from the folds of Mungo's robe.

Then, chillingly, Zorn's laughter ceased as abruptly as it had begun. 'So, Mungo the Great,' he snarled, his words sounding as though they were coming from within a vast cavern, 'you gave the game away, didn't you? After all this time, you couldn't resist the temptation to show off with one of your pathetic little tricks, could you? Yes,' Zorn rasped, 'you gave the game away, and now I've found you – at last!'

Mungo was unable to hide his loathing. 'You'll still rot in that foul hell hole,' he growled. 'You'll rot there with the rest of your kind – forever!'

Zorn's claw-like hand appeared beside his face, and from his fingers Jasper was dangling by the tail, struggling hopelessly, squealing in terror. 'If anyone is going to rot,' Zorn boomed, 'it is you, Mungo!' Then, smirking, he diverted his stare towards the wriggling mouse. 'There's not much of him, but lightly grilled with some rat livers … hmm, and a nice bottle of Chianti…' Zorn smacked his lips, the sound of his manic laughter echoing out once more as he and his enveloping cloud disappeared in a puff of green smoke.

Mungo and the children were left standing in a

still, eerie silence.

Jamie was staring up at Mungo, his eyes moist with tears. 'Can I have my mouse back now?' he asked.

Mungo remained silent, but the look on his face suggested that he wasn't sure the little boy's request would be an easy one to satisfy.

'Wh-who was that horrible man?' Susie stuttered as she crept from the sanctuary of Mungo's robe.

The old man slumped into his rocking chair, his expression grave. 'That was Zorn. The Lord of Goblin Hall, he calls himself. Hmm, and Genghis Khan was a pussy cat compared to that evil guffbag.'

A puzzled frown wrinkled Susie's brow. 'Goblin Hall? You mean...?

'Yes, the old castle there. Goblin Ha', as the locals hereabout refer to it.' Mungo gestured across the glen towards the woods, where the crumbling remains of a large building were just visible through the trees.

'But nobody lives there,' Susie pooh-poohed. 'It's a dump. Only a heap of silly old stones.'

Mungo shook his head. 'Ah, well, it may seem that way now, but –'

'I'm going to get Jasper back,' Jamie butted in, and made to head off towards the ruins.

Mungo stood up quickly and grabbed his arm. 'No, boy! You must never go near that castle. Nor you,' he went on, turning to Susie. 'Not now. Not any more.' He stared over the glen with a troubled look in his eyes. 'That would only be playing into Zorn's hands.'

'But Jasper,' Jamie protested. 'I want Jasper back.'

Sighing, Mungo patted the little boy's shoulder. 'Don't fret, I'll get you another mouse.' Then, with a reassuring little chuckle, he added, 'Maybe one that does tricks, hmm?'

But Jamie was having none of it. 'No, I'm going to get Jasper!' he insisted, and prepared to head off again.

Once more, Mungo reached out and stopped him. 'Wait!' he said, his tone kindly but firm. Over the top of his spectacles, he looked at both children in turn, reading their expressions. He could see that they didn't understand, couldn't possibly understand, the danger they might now be in. 'Come,' he smiled, sitting back down on his rocking chair and beckoning the children to join him. 'I think I must tell you a story.'

Though Susie and Jamie knew it would be going against their mother's wishes, curiosity got the better of them. So, without further ado, they hunkered down cross-legged in front of Mungo's chair.

'Bet I've heard it before,' Susie grumped, not wishing to appear too interested.

Mungo turned a deaf ear and made himself comfortable. 'Now,' he began, 'this happened a long, long time ago – many centuries in the past, when I was but a lad, and when the castle of Goblin Hall was at its most magnificent – the grandest castle in the land, the home of the Master, the Great High Sorcerer himself...'

* * * * *

– CHAPTER THREE –

THE YEAR 750 AD –
THE CASTLE OF GOBLIN HALL...

The great hall of the castle was buzzing with activity. Groups of long-robed trainee wizards and witches, all in their early teens, were gathered round wooden benches arranged in rows under the cavernous roof. Some of these sorcery students were carefully copying notes from bulky, leather-bound books that breathed out little wisps of dust every time a page was turned. Others were busy brewing up steaming potions in all manner of beakers and cauldrons, while yet others were making objects and creatures appear and disappear in whiffs of smoke.

Watching them carefully as he wandered slowly up and down the hall was the Master, a very old man, with long white hair and matching beard. He was dressed in a flowing cloak imprinted with mystic symbols, and was carrying a tall, slender staff of intricately carved wood. Occasionally, he would pause to offer a quiet word of advice to any of his young charges who needed it, or a sharp reprimand to those who deserved it.

On a minstrel gallery overlooking this industrious scene was a band of six goblins, cheery-looking little fellows, with big, pointed ears, and faces that were broader than they were long, giving them the appearance of smiling pumpkin lanterns. They were clad in tartan, and playing curious musical instruments to produce what sounded like some sort of medieval pop music. The inclusion of a set of bagpipes added a Scottish flavour to the overall effect. On their drummer's bass drum skin was printed *THE KILTIES*. Other pint-sized goblins were scurrying about the floor of the hall, happily helping the students with their experiments, or running errands to the apothecary's store.

Standing alone at one bench was a lad behaving in a distinctly flustered way. He seemed to be having trouble making a bored-looking piglet do something it didn't want to. The Master, meanwhile, was watching from a discreet distance, smiling knowingly.

'Now, let's get this right,' the lad muttered to himself, glancing sideways at a bulky volume, while pointing the spread fingers of one hand at the piglet. The book was open at a page headed '*Spells For Basic Levitation*', and sub-titled '*Pigs* Will *Fly*!' The young trainee wizard then focused his attention on the piglet, looking deep into its eyes. 'All right – this time!' the lad mumbled. 'Here we go...' He inhaled deeply, took a final quick glance at the book, then shouted, '*Balganab zinabbo*! *FLY*!'

The piglet, still standing four-square on the bench, gave a derisory grunt and shot the lad a what-a-useless-nitwit look. The student scratched the back of his head, looking first at the piglet, then forlornly at the open book of spells.

The Master's smile widened as he approached the bench. 'No, no, no, that will never work, laddie,' he said. 'It's not *"Balganab"*, nor indeed *"zinabbo"*.' He pointed at the book with his staff. 'Regard the writings. See, the spell is clearly inscribed.'

Looking more than a little confused, the young trainee silently mouthed the written words.

The Master watched him for a few moments, then enquired, 'You *can* read, can't you, laddie?'

'Why, y-yes, in ten languages, Master.'

The Master appeared less than convinced. 'Hmm,' he nodded, 'then you will see that the spell reads, not *"Balganab zinabbo"*, but *"Baglanagab zibanno"*. No?'

The student squinted at the book, nervously fiddling with his chin while muttering the words to himself again.

His patience exhausted, the Master shooed him aside. 'Here, allow me to demonstrate. First of all you must appear confident – *be* confident.' He made a vague, almost dismissive gesture towards the piglet. 'Or else the object creature will never obey. Observe.' Feet slightly apart, he set his stance firmly, loosening his shoulders, his eyes fixed on the piglet. He then raised his staff and pointed it at the little animal in a manner akin to a matador about to dispatch a bull with his sword. '*O-o-o-oh, baglan-baglan-baglan,*' he chanted, before finally shouting, '*Ooblan, porko! Baglanagab zibanno! FLY!*'

Flapping wings instantly burst from the shoulders of the piglet, who, with an apprehensive smile tugging at the corner of his mouth, rose into the air, and was soon swooping like a fat, pink swallow high above the students. With all traces of his initial anxiety now dispelled, the piglet was grinning delightedly.

'Gee, what a totally awesome buzz, man!' he hollered in a slow, American drawl, before executing a perfect figure-of-eight.

The lad stared up at him in amazement.

His face expressionless, the Master raised his staff in the direction of the soaring porker and called out, '*Volaragab terminabbo!*'

As a result, the piglet came sweeping down and landed on the bench, his wings disappearing as quickly as they had appeared. 'Wow! Cool trip!' he enthused. 'Yeah, I'd give a week's swill ration for another go at that!'

The Master looked at his young student with raised eyebrows. 'Well, laddie, you heard what the creature said...'

The lad fidgeted, clearly uneasy about exposing his faltering skills to the Master's scrutiny yet again.

But the Master was unbending. He motioned him to get on with it.

'Come on, kid' the piglet urged. 'Do like the boss man says, will ya! Quit dawdlin' and get me airborne again!'

With a wan smile at the Master, the lad took another peek at the spell book, then, fingers spread, pointed his hand at the piglet.

Keenly shuffling his trotters, the little porker braced himself. 'Alrightee,' he muttered, teeth clenched. 'Ten seconds to blast-off! Ten, nine...'

As the piglet continued his countdown, the student closed his eyes, his face a study in total concentration. *'Baglan-baglan-baglan,'* he intoned, his voice getting steadily louder. *'Ooblan porko! Baglanagab zibanno! FLY!'*

'...one, zero!' the piglet called out, while flapping wings sprouted from his shoulders, lifting him slowly from the bench in a near perfect take-off. 'Yeah!' he yelled. 'We are go for Earth orbit, Houston! Eat my dust, baby!'

When the lad opened his eyes, he could hardly believe what he was seeing.

The Master allowed himself a smile of quiet satisfaction as he watched the piglet perform some over-confident aerobatics high up near the ceiling. 'There you are, laddie,' he said to his apprentice. 'Easy when you know how, no?'

But the lad was too pleased with himself to reply. Instead, he stared up at the flying piglet, grinning, nodding his head in silent approbation as the little animal looped the loop while blowing raspberries to mimic the sound of an aeroplane engine.

Clearly impressed, the Master patted his young student's back. 'Well, well,' he smiled, 'you appear to have a particular talent for this art, my boy.' He pointed his staff ceilingward. 'Look, the swineling now performs like a flying machine.'

'Amazing,' the lad gasped, unable to take his eyes off the little pig.

'Amazing indeed,' the Master muttered under his breath, 'since flying machines have yet to be invented.'

'Mmm, absolutely,' his protégé mumbled, too

fascinated by the piglet's aerial display to take in what his mentor had said.

While the lad continued to gaze up at the zooming porker, the Master looked at his pupil closely, weighing him up, assessing his potential. 'Tell me,' he said at length, 'what name do they call you by, my boy?'

Not wanting to miss the merest detail of the ongoing performance above them, the lad glanced briefly at the Master and said, 'Me? Oh, my name is Mungo, sire.'

'Well, young Mungo, I shall be watching your progress with much interest from now on. Ah yes,' he nodded, 'we must develop this gift of yours. Very rare, you know.'

The Master's compliment snapped Mungo out of his preoccupation with the piglet's stunts. He looked at his superior with a little frown of disbelief. 'Me? A gift? Oh, but this – well, it's the first time I've managed to – I mean, nothing usually happens when I…'

'Aha, but that's the very thing, young Mungo.' The Master motioned towards the flying piglet. 'To make an earthbound creature perform so spectacularly as this on your first successful act of levitation is rare indeed, believe me.'

The piglet was now showing off by noisily buzzing the other students, skimming over their heads at breakneck speed and causing their candles to gutter in his slipstream. Even so, most of the students ignored him completely, well accustomed as they were to seeing the bizarre antics of all kinds of spellbound animals during their everyday studies. Only one or two even bothered to cast him bored, get-lost looks, which the piglet, in turn, chose to totally ignore.

Young Mungo, meanwhile, was still trying to come to terms with the Master's unexpected praise. 'A gift? Me? I didn't realise – I mean, well, thank you, sire. I – I –'

The Master laid a calming hand on his shoulder. 'But lest my compliments swell your head, laddie, perhaps you should now demonstrate to me how you can return that insufferable piece of flying ham safely back to terra firma.'

They looked up to where the piglet was now flitting about above the minstrel gallery, giggling to himself and making his aeroplane noises. The Kiltie musicians, still playing their instruments, pretended to pay him no heed, though the scowls on their faces indicated that they were becoming more than a little irritated by his presence.

'Hey, funky sounds, guys!' the piglet called to the Kilties as he hovered over their heads, beating time to their music with one of his front trotters. 'Yeah, real groovy!'

'Oink off, bacon bird!' the drummer snarled back. 'You're creating a draught – *and* you smell!'

The Master, sensing trouble, told Mungo that his 'object creature' would do well not to invoke the wrath of the Kilties. 'They are good-natured wee fellows, certainly, but not known to suffer such exhibitionists gladly.'

While looping another loop, the piglet shouted, 'Hey, sure as apple sauce is apple sauce, this beats the truffles outta rootlin' in the mud any old day! Pigs might fly, ya say? Yeah, just call me the second Wilbur – right? *Whee-ee-ee!*'

A look of puzzlement came to young Mungo's face. He turned to the Master. 'The *second* Wilbur – right? Who is the first one?'

The Master pulled a shrug. 'Oh, just a mortal – a levitator – in a place to be called America.' He shook his head dismissively. 'But that's all in the future, and you must concern yourself only with the present, my boy. One thing at a time, yes?'

Mungo's interest had been aroused, though. 'This Wilbur the levitator, who belongs in a place that doesn't yet exist … are you saying that piglet up there can see the future?'

The Master hunched his shoulders again, thought for a moment, then said with a wry smile, 'Some might suggest a flying pig is capable of just about anything, no?' He watched Mungo's look of puzzlement deepen, gave a little chuckle, then patted him on the hand. 'But come, laddie, do not pollute your mind with such idle conundrums. Concentrate only on the task in hand. You, uh, have a piglet to gravitate, I believe?'

'Hmm,' Mungo frowned, his puzzled look graduating to one of panic. He glanced sidelong at the spell book, running his forefinger over the page, then closed his eyes while trying to memorise the prescribed incantation.

'Come on, my boy,' the Master goaded. 'I haven't got an entire millennium to wait, you know!'

Mungo raised his eyes to the piglet, pointed at it with

his right hand, spread his fingers in the required way, steadied himself, then shouted, '*VOLARAGAB TERMINABBO-O-OH*!'

Instantly, the piglet began a downward glide, albeit clearly against his will. He looked round at his extended wings and, his tail uncurling with the effort, strained with all his might to flap them. But without success.

The Master gave young Mungo a hearty slap on the back. 'Well done, lad! Well done!'

Smiling weakly, Mungo crossed his fingers behind his back – a gesture which did not go unnoticed by the Master.

'Aw, hey, don't be a party pooper, man!' the piglet called to Mungo. 'I was just startin' to have a real ball up here, for cryin' out loud!'

On the minstrel gallery, the Kiltie musicians winked at each other. As Wilbur the piglet, thrusting his legs forward for the landing, glided at speed towards young Mungo's bench, the Kilties jerked their heads in his direction. This action coincided with a short twanging sound, and Wilbur was propelled forward at even greater speed, overshooting the bench and heading straight for the nearest wall.

'*WOA-A-AH*!' he yelled.

Mungo was left to look on helplessly as his first feat of animal levitation began to go horribly wrong. Conversely, the Kiltie musicians were delighted. They were still playing their instruments, but grinning at each other in anticipation of the piglet's imminent and, in their opinion, thoroughly deserved downfall. Young Mungo crossed his fingers even more tightly and offered up a silent prayer. But to no avail.

Wilbur, suddenly wingless again, tumbled to a clattering halt among a heap of buckets and baskets in the corner of the hall. An explosion of giggling erupted on the Kilties' gallery, while even the most disinterested of students finally looked up from their experiments, pointed to the crash site and laughed their heads off.

Young Mungo was distraught. Totally crestfallen, he stared towards the piglet, who, although apparently unharmed, was lying on his back, kicking the air in a desperate attempt to get up and regain a modicum of dignity – if indeed he'd ever had any.

The Master cast a mildly reproachful glance at the Kiltie musicians, knowing full well, though Mungo didn't, that their mischief had been responsible for this comic catastrophe. 'Let that be a lesson to you,' he said to Mungo, then indicated his apprentice's tightly-crossed fingers. 'And never forget, laddie, that there is no harm in hoping for the best, but never take it for granted.'

Suitably chastened, Mungo dipped his head.

Back on all fours, Wilbur gave himself a shake and stepped from the tangle of debris, *his* reaction clearly more of annoyance than embarrassment. 'Jeez, what a total bummer!' he grunted out of the corner of his mouth.

With a renewed look of puzzlement, Young Mungo addressed the Master. 'Bummer, party pooper, funky, groovy? He speaks in a strange tongue, this little animal, does he not, sire?'

The Master nodded sagely. 'Hmm, it will be called American,' he said, then shrugged in a resigned sort of way. 'The creature not only sees the future, but also talks it, I'm afraid.'

Mungo heaved a heavy sigh and stared pensively at the strutting piglet. 'I fear I still have much to learn, Master.'

'And so you will,' the Master replied. 'And so you will, my boy.'

* * * * *

– CHAPTER FOUR –

BACK TO THE PRESENT –
OUTSIDE OLD MUNGO'S COTTAGE...

'And so I did,' old Mungo told Susie and Jamie. 'I did indeed learn much, and all from the Master, the Great High Sorcerer himself. Ah yes, for he took a special interest in my progress from that day on, you see. Hmm, oddly, despite my, uh, *slight* miscalculation of the trajectory of the flying piglet's return to my work table, the Master thought I had shown great potential as a –'

'But what happened to the piglet?' Susie demanded, not interested in hearing any more of the old man's personal history, for the present at least.

Her unexpected interruption knocked Mungo completely out of his stride. 'What? Oh, the piglet,' he flustered. 'He, well, I think he's still around somewhere. Yes, acting in films these days, I'm told. The, ehm, *movies*, as you call them.' Old Mungo pondered this for a moment, then mumbled, 'Though what dramatic roles there could possibly be for a talking pig is beyond my comprehension.'

Jamie's draw dropped. 'Babe!' he whispered,

wonder-struck.

'No, silly!' Susie tutted. 'Wilbur would be too old. Babe's still a baby.' She turned to Mungo and stated bluntly, 'I mean, Wilbur the flying piglet – he must be *really* ancient by now. Just like you.'

Mungo feigned a little smile, trying gamely to give the impression that Susie's comment hadn't miffed him. 'Ancient? Well, no – not really. They, uhm, tend not to look their age, once they've been spellbound … piglets, that is.' He cleared his throat and set about changing the subject. 'Yes, well, anyway – as I was about to say...'

'But what happened to the pretty castle?' Jamie asked, pointing to the ruins on the other side of the glen.

'Ah, yes indeed, boy – that's *exactly* what I was about to say!' said Mungo, glad to be reminded.

'Can't believe *that* old dump was ever a fairytale castle like Snow White's,' Susie muttered.

'Aha, but it was,' Mungo assured her. 'Even more magnificent, in fact. Yes, and it also had many more dwarfs than Snow White did.'

Confused, the two children glanced at each other, then glowered at the old man.

'Dwarfs?' Jamie queried.

'And more than *seven* of them?' Susie checked.

'Absolutely!' Mungo grinned. 'All those Kiltie goblins I told you about. There were droves of them, you see. Which, of course, was why the castle was called Goblin Hall in the first place.' He paused, then added with an impish smile, 'As I'm sure you had already worked out for yourselves, yes?'

'No,' Jamie freely admitted.

'But I had,' Susie haughtily fibbed.

It didn't really matter either way, because Mungo's thoughts were already drifting off. A faraway look came to his eyes as he gazed across at the sad remains of the castle. 'Oh yes, it was quite magnificent when I was a lad,' he murmured wistfully. 'Quite magnificent – until that fateful day, many years later…'

* * *

THE YEAR 987 AD –
NEAR THE CASTLE OF GOBLIN HALL…

Looking down from the little hill with the dead tree on top, it would have been hard to imagine a more enchanting scene. The turreted splendour of Goblin Hall rose up from a land of rolling meadows, on which a herd of deer grazed by a gently winding stream. But for the sound of birdsong in the greenwood round the castle and the muted tinkling of sheep bells on the hillsides beyond, nothing stirred in the warm morning air.

Mungo, now with the look of a young man in his early twenties, though still dressed in the apprentice's robes he wore over two centuries before, was approaching the summit of the little hill. With him was the Master, who now appeared extremely old and frail as he struggled up the final few paces, using his long staff as a support.

Although they didn't know it, they were being

watched from behind the dead tree by two Keelies, goblins of similar size to the Kilties, but with evil, mean-looking faces, their top lips adorned with drooping moustaches matted with grease. They were dressed in sleeveless tunics made from rat skin, and woolly leggings criss-crossed with leather thongs, which lent them the appearance of miniature Viking raiders. On their heads they wore skull-hugging iron helmets, with two little horns attached to accentuate the devilish image that set this tribe of goblins apart from all the others.

The two Keelies ducked well out of sight as the Master, exhausted by the climb, reached the dead tree and leaned a hand against it.

'Phew!' he panted. 'I – I thought I'd never make it.'

Mungo indicated a nearby rock. 'Come, sit here, sire. Rest a moment.' He took the Master by the elbow and helped him ease his stiff old bones down onto the stone.

'A-a-ah, that's better!' the elderly wizard puffed. 'By the stars, laddie, I – I'm beginning to feel my age.'

'And what age would that be?' Mungo asked with a twinkle in his eyes.

The Master swatted the air dismissively. 'Who knows? Birthdays … I stopped counting those things after a thousand or so.'

Young Mungo gave a little laugh. 'Then I think you climb very well, sire … all things considered.'

'Hmmff! It would have been easier just to magic myself up here as usual, but that know-it-all young physician of mine says I need the exercise. Puh! A fine lot of good exercise will do me now. More liable to kill me, I'd say.' Breathing more freely now, the Master looked up at Mungo and declared, 'I tell you, laddie, we wizards were healthier when we cured ourselves with the tried and tested old spells. Now these new-fangled medicine men – mumbo-jumbo potion-pushers and leech-feeders, I call them – have muscled in on things and tell us we need more exercise. Physicians?' He swatted the air again. 'Pah! We were better off without them!'

Prudently, Mungo inclined his head in apparent agreement, then silently looked out towards the castle and its idyllic surroundings, leaving the Master to mutter away grumpily to himself for a while.

'This truly is a beautiful place,' Mungo eventually remarked.

'Yes, indeed it is,' the Master sighed, 'and I will sorely miss it, my boy.'

Mungo turned round to face his elderly mentor. 'Miss it? But why? I don't understand what you –'

The Master held up a hand. 'It is time, young Mungo. Time for me to go to the Higher Place.'

Behind the dead tree, the two Keelies exchanged intrigued glances. Here was a juicy morsel of news they hadn't expected to pick up.

But young Mungo still didn't understand what the Master had meant. Or perhaps he just didn't really *want* to understand. For he had forged such a strong bond with this kindly and wise old man over the years that he couldn't bear to contemplate life without him. 'The Higher Place?' he repeated. 'But, sire, I – '

The Master interrupted him with a soothing smile.

'Do not worry, my boy. Do not sadden yourself for me. It is the way, and none can change it. And truly, I am content that my time has come.' He fell silent and gazed dreamily across the glen. 'Though, yes,' he said after a while, 'I shall miss this place ... very, very much.'

With tears welling in his eyes, Mungo shook his head, hoping against hope that the Master didn't really mean what he was saying. 'But without you,' he implored, 'how can we...?'

His words faded away as the Master smiled up at him again. It was a gentle, reassuring smile, but tinged with a look of finality that told Mungo it would be pointless to say anything more. He knew the rules of the Brotherhood well enough. The Master's time had come. It was the way, and none could change it.

The old wizard laid a hand on Mungo's. 'I have taught you all I can, my boy,' he said gravely, though with a glint of humour his eyes. 'Not all I *know* – but all I *can*.'

Lost for words, Mungo could only offer a sad smile.

A serious look returned to the Master's face. 'The rest you must learn by yourself, through mistakes, through experience – just as I had to.'

'Yes, I do understand that, sire, and I am deeply grateful to you for all you have taught me. But without *you*, the Great High Sorcerer, who is to teach the young ones? Who is to guide them in the way you have guided me?'

The Keelies cocked their pointed ears, doubly intrigued now.

A serene smile lit the Master's face. 'That is why, my boy, I am content that my time to go to the Higher Place has come.'

Mungo shook his head again, a frown of confusion on his brow.

'For you,' the Master continued, '– you, Mungo, are now ready.'

'Ready? I – I do not understand...'

'But it is simple,' the Master shrugged. 'You have worked hard over the long years to learn the ancient arts, and now, as is the way, you must pass that knowledge down to the young ones, just as I have passed my knowledge down to you.'

Mungo was totally taken aback, shocked, scared even, by what he had just been told. Like many a hopeful young wizard, he had allowed himself to dream at times about one day attaining the highest office in the Brotherhood of Sorcerers. But it had only ever been a dream – and a wild one at that.

'No, no, Master, I cannot,' he objected. 'I cannot take your place.' A feeling of panic was building up inside him. 'It – it would be impossible, for I do not yet possess the –'

'It is decided,' the Master insisted. 'It has been decreed in the Higher Place that you will succeed me, and that is how it will be – how it *must* be. It *is* the way.'

Behind the dead tree, the two Keelies grimaced. They didn't like the sound of this one little bit.

His thoughts in disarray, young Mungo slumped down onto the rock beside the Master, staring at the ground in disbelief.

The Master fully understood the mental anguish the young fellow was experiencing. He watched him closely for a few moments, then, handing him his staff, said, 'Do not be afraid, my son.'

Young Mungo looked at the Master, then at the staff.

'Take it,' the Master urged. 'Hold it.'

Hesitantly, young Mungo took the staff in his hands and gazed at it in awe.

'The staff of the Great High Sorcerer,' the Master continued, his expression solemn now. 'Older than time itself.' He gestured towards the dead tree under which they were sitting. 'The staff was cut from the ancient Tree of Knowledge, from whose seed this tree alone survives.'

The Master's revelation surprised and fascinated Mungo in equal measure. He patted the tree's gnarled trunk. 'You mean this, the old Lightning Tree, has some kind of connection with the Great High Sorcerer's staff?'

'Indeed. For through its roots flows the Power, the very stuff on which our mystic energies feed.' The Master raised his eyes. 'And its branches point to the Higher Place, and from there they receive strength and inspiration for the member of our Brotherhood who stands here below ... while holding this ancient staff, the key to the Power.'

Young Mungo was becoming more confused. 'But – but, sire, I thought the castle, Goblin Hall, was the sacred place, the source...'

The Master shook his head. 'The castle is but a seat of learning, built there by our forefathers to be close to this hill, this tree, the true fountainhead of the Power.'

Young Mungo stared at the staff again, his expression blank. He felt overwhelmed and totally undeserving of the great responsibility with which he was being entrusted.

'Come, my son,' the Master said, taking hold of Mungo's arm to steady himself. 'Hand me the staff. Oh yes indeed,' he chuckled, 'for all its wondrous powers, its greatest use to me these days is often as a walking stick.'

Mungo gently helped the old man to his feet.

'A-a-ah, oh, that's it!' the Master panted as he straightened his stiff old limbs. 'Now, let us be off, my boy. We must prepare for the ceremony.'

Mungo canted his head. 'The, ehm ... *ceremony*?'

'Why, yes!' the Master beamed. 'Your inauguration as the new High Sorcerer. And this very night at that!'

Gasps of astonishment rose from the Keelies' hiding place. Startled by the sound, young Mungo stepped cautiously round the tree, where the two evil goblins stood facing him up, their faces twisted into snarls of hatred.

The only reaction their posturing drew from Mungo was a mocking laugh. 'Hah, Keelies!' he scoffed. 'Spying for your master, eh?' He made a shooing flick of his hand. 'Begone, insignificant freaks! Go on, crawl back under your stones, you ugly little slugs!'

But the Keelies weren't to be that easily seen off. Although tiny, they were, like their more agreeable Kiltie cousins, gutsy little fellows when presented with a challenge. They pointed at Mungo, hissing menacingly while firing miniature bolts of lightning from their fingertips.

Mungo laughed again as he parried the shots with his forearm. He thrust out his hand, fingers spread in the customary way.

Cringing, The Keelies crept back, clutching each other.

'Away with you!' Mungo shouted. 'Away! Or, by the stars, I'll turn you into lumps of cow dung!'

The Keelies screamed in panic, then jumped into the air and disappeared in little puffs of green smoke.

Young Mungo held his sides laughing. But the Master didn't appear in the least amused when Mungo joined him to start the descent of the hill. 'We know where that pair of nasty little trolls are headed,' he said with a grim look.

'Hmm, straight to Zorn,' Mungo murmured, the smile fading from his face as the potential gravity of the situation began to dawn on him.

'And,' the Master continued, 'he won't be happy when they tell him what they've just overheard.'

Mungo stroked his chin. 'Yes, I've heard it said that Zorn has always claimed that he should be the one to take your place, when – when your time came to...' He found himself unable to speak the heart-breaking words.

'And so he would have,' the Master confirmed, 'except that mere magic was never enough for Zorn, for he had this overwhelming urge to dabble in the black arts. And it didn't matter that I warned him many times over the centuries.' He shook his head in despair. 'No, he was determined, *driven* it seemed, to delve into the dark mysteries of the forbidden crafts.'

Young Mungo fell silent, thinking deeply. 'But in fairness to Zorn,' he said at length, 'he *is* older, more experienced by far than I am. Perhaps, sire, if he renounced his interest in the forbidden crafts, he – well, he *might* yet be able to take his place as your rightful successor?'

The Master shook his head again, but resolutely this time. 'It can never be. By his own ill-judged actions, Zorn forfeited long ago any right he might have had to that heritage.'

'But his skills,' young Mungo protested, '– they are much greater than mine. The Power too. I mean, everyone knows that the strength of the Power in Zorn surpasses by far its strength in me.'

The Master stopped and looked Mungo in the eye. 'Ah, but you forget, my boy, that the staff – this ancient staff – will be yours. And, with this in your hand, you need fear no-one ... not even Zorn and all the evil he has chosen to embody.'

Though he didn't doubt that the Master was telling the truth, young Mungo still worried. He knew full well that Zorn would be a formidable enemy, and devious too, if he chose to be. And it was certain his anger would be intense for being denied the exalted position he coveted so much. Mungo sighed. Whatever happened now would be beyond his control. Thanks to the eavesdropping Keelies, Zorn would already have been forewarned, which inevitably meant forearmed. The young wizard's emotions were in a muddle. His stomach was already churning at the thought of the enormous responsibility about to be thrust on his shoulders, his joy at being elevated to the position of Great High Sorcerer tempered by the threat to his very life that such an honour might bring.

The Master took his arm. 'Come, my son. We have much to do before the commencement of the ceremony...'

* * * * *

– CHAPTER FIVE –

THE PRESENT DAY –
OUTSIDE OLD MUNGO'S COTTAGE...

Susie and Jamie were now totally captivated by Mungo's tale. Even Charlie the dog had ventured out from his hiding place to join them, sitting on the grass, staring up at the old man rocking gently in his chair as he spoke.

'So, that night,' Mungo continued, 'wizards, warlocks and witches and, uhm, of course, their various attendants and familiars came from all over the world and gathered in the great throne room of Goblin Hall Castle.'

'Did the witches come on broomsticks?' Susie asked.

'No, no, girl.' Mungo chuckled at the very idea. 'No, I'm afraid broomsticks are only for fairy tales, you know. Far too slow and uncomfortable for travel in the real supernatural world. Broomsticks? Mmm,' he frowned, '– only fit for sweeping floors, in my humble opinion.'

'So how *do* they travel?' Susie pressed.

'Witches and wizards? Easy! A pop of the fingers,

and "*Zibanno*!" – you're wherever you want to be.'

Jamie, clearly impressed by the notion of this nifty mode of transport, looked down at the fingers of his right hand, attempted to pop them (though not too successfully), then called out, '*ZIBANNO*!' Next, he looked down at his body, quickly surveyed his surroundings, then observed with undisguised disappointment, 'I'm still here!'

'That's 'cause you're not a wizard, silly,' Susie giggled.

Mungo laughed and tousled Jamie's hair. 'Where did you want to go to anyway, boy?'

Jamie scowled and lowered his head. 'To where Jasper's at.'

Mungo managed a sheepish smile, but elected to remain silent on the subject of Jamie's evaporated mouse.

'Anyway,' Susie piped up, now doubly keen to hear more of old Mungo's story, 'what happened next at the ceremony?'

'Next? Oh, yes – next.' Mungo settled back in his rocking chair. 'Well, there they all were, the elite of the world's sorcerous fraternity. Oh,' he added with a respectful nod to Susie, 'and, indeed, sorority – all dressed in their finest, and assembled within the priceless magnificence of Goblin Hall...'

* * *

THE YEAR 987 AD - GOBLIN HALL CASTLE...

The castle's vast throne room was the last word in

grandeur: a somewhat bizarre grandeur, no doubt, but grandeur nonetheless. Protruding from the high, vaulted ceiling were rows of stuffed dragons' heads, and from their gaping jaws were suspended long pennants. These were lavishly embroidered with live snakes, whose constant slithering and wriggling wove ever-changing patterns on the heavy silk material. Each pennant represented the home country of one of the hundreds of mystic guests gathered there to witness the inauguration of young Mungo as their absolute superior. Around the walls hung life-size portraits of all previous Great High Sorcerers. Magically, the subject of every painting had the ability to move within the confines of his own gilt frame, and to converse freely with grotesque but seemingly good-natured gargoyles, carved in stone on either side.

The floor of the great hall, which had been carpeted for the occasion in millions of fresh dandelion petals, was teeming with wizards, witches, warlocks, elves and goblins of every colour, shape and size. Everyone was dressed in weird and wonderful finery befitting such a weird and wonderful event. They, the aristocracy of the world of white magic, were milling around, exchanging greetings, bowing, talking, whispering, gossiping. Some were comparing new tricks and spells, while others – particularly those entitled to wear tall, pointed hats – were merely meandering slowly through the throng, looking superior and suitably aloof. In any event, the atmosphere was highly charged, the tension building as the start of a once-in-many-lifetimes experience for everyone drew ever closer.

A golden throne, flanked by two live phoenix birds, sat on a raised platform at the far end of the hall. On a gallery above, a small orchestra of Kilties was playing stately-but-funky music on unicorn-horn flutes and fiddles made from clam shells, all of which added to the sense of occasion in an appropriately quirky way. Suddenly, the music stopped. A drum roll sounded, and an expectant hush fell over the gathered company. Four Kiltie trumpeters then stepped to the front of the gallery and blared out a fanfare.

This directed everyone's attention towards the great double doors at the opposite end of the chamber, where stood the Master, staff in hand. He wore a crown jewelled with glow-worms, and was dressed in robes woven from silky-blue mermaid's hair that flowed into a long, peacock-feather train carried by six Kiltie courtiers. The assembled guests fell respectfully back to leave an aisle running all the way from the doorway to the throne. On a discreet signal from the Master, the orchestra and trumpeters struck up a stately slow-march. After a dramatic pause, the old head wizard commenced his final grand parade, followed by a nervous-looking young Mungo, who was also dressed in ceremonial attire, though noticeably less elaborate than that of his superior.

The little procession made its way, step by sedate step, through the hall, the Master nodding majestically to his subjects, who bowed in reverence as he passed. Young Mungo, on the other hand, flashed little self-conscious smiles to his peers, painfully aware that he was being weighed up meticulously by each and every one of them.

'Sure an' if he isn't terrible young for such an important job an' all,' he heard one green-skinned leprechaun whisper to a web-footed water sprite.

'And a bit on the skinny side,' remarked a turban-wearing genie, who would have made a sumo wrestler look slim.

'Nice eyes, though,' a particularly wizened old witch croaked lecherously. 'Hmm ... waggles his bum nicely too.'

After what had become a seemingly endless ordeal for Mungo, the Master finally reached the dais and lowered himself stiffly onto the throne. The Kiltie attendants arranged his train neatly on the floor by his feet, before stepping back to take up position behind the two phoenix birds.

Mungo halted a pace away, bowed to the Master, then got down on one knee and looked up at him through apprehensive eyes.

Right on cue, the orchestra and trumpeters stopped playing. An intense silence settled upon the great room. You could have heard a flea sneeze as all eyes focused on the two central characters in the forthcoming ceremony. Mungo's heart was thumping, his entire body trembling.

'We are gathered here,' the Master proclaimed, his voice reverberating around the stone walls, 'for the investiture of Mungo, the brother who kneels here before me, as my successor to the exalted office of Great High Sorcerer.'

As one, the gathered company dipped their heads. 'So be it, Master' they chanted. 'So be it.'

'For it has been ordained in the Higher Place,' the Master declared, 'that this sacred staff I hold in my hand shall be passed to our brother Mungo. And he shall be the keeper of the staff and the guardian of its secrets and the holder of its Power from this day, until he, in turn, is called to rise up to the Higher Place.'

The congregation dipped their heads once more. 'So be it, Master,' they repeated. 'So be it.'

'And,' the Master went on, 'if there is anyone among you who knows of any reason why this should not be, declare that knowledge now, or forever hold your peace.' The old man cast his eyes over the sea of faces gazing up at him, then got slowly to his feet and addressed Mungo: 'Are you ready to take the solemn oath, my son?'

Mungo swallowed hard, his mouth as dry as sawdust. 'I – I am, sire,' he stated as firmly as he could, though hardly recognising the sound of his own voice.

'Then bow your head.'

Mungo did as instructed.

The Master lowered the end of his staff onto his young successor's shoulder, closed his eyes and inclined his face upwards. 'Oh, Mighty One, who rules supreme in the Higher Place, bear witness to our brother's pledge to you. For by his troth, he –'

But his incantation was interrupted by a loud clatter as the great doors at the far end of the chamber crashed open. The assembled guests turned their heads towards the noise. And there was Zorn, standing in the doorway, arms akimbo, legs apart, his expression dark and threatening. He was dressed, like the six Keelie henchmen escorting him, in the garb of a marauding Viking, except that the horns on his helmet were significantly longer than the Keelies', and a black cloak resembling a bat's wings hung grotesquely from his shoulders.

Startled and confused by the commotion, Mungo got to his feet and turned to face the door.

'You have no place here!' the Master called out to Zorn.

'It is *I* who should be taking your place!' Zorn snapped back. 'It is my right!'

'You have no such right, and you violate the sanctity of this occasion by your very presence!'

Zorn, his eyes ablaze with fury, raised his hand and released a lightning bolt, which shot from his claw-like fingertips and exploded at the Master's feet.

'I challenge you,' he yelled, 'for that *is* my right!'

'*No*-one can challenge the Great High Sorcerer!' the Master retorted.

'But I *can* challenge your toady underling, the upstart Mungo who stands before you!'

The Master shook his head. 'The time to object has passed. It is too late to speak or act against –'

'I challenge *you*, Mungo!' Zorn roared, cutting the Master off. 'It will be your magical powers against mine, and the winner takes all!'

'No! I forbid it!' the Master shouted over gasps of astonishment from the vast gathering.

Mungo half turned towards the Master, determined

to appear deserving of his impending promotion, despite a gnawing lack of self-belief. 'Please, sire,' he pleaded, 'if I am to take your place, I must show my worth now.'

Zorn let out a scornful laugh. 'Ha! So the toad sprouts fangs, eh?'

The Master leaned towards Mungo and whispered behind a cupped hand, 'But if you lose, my boy, Zorn will –'

'I cannot lose,' Mungo butted in, faking an air of confidence so convincingly that he almost convinced himself, 'for I will be holding the staff.'

'Well, Mungo the Great,' Zorn taunted from the other end of the hall, 'do you accept my challenge? Or is your strength limited to your tongue?' Then, to impress his attendant Keelies, he added sarcastically, 'As a toad catches flies, perhaps?'

The Keelies joined Zorn in an outburst of mocking laughter. His pride hurt, Mungo narrowed his eyes and carefully aimed the outstretched fingers of his hand at Zorn's gang of jeering goblins.

'*Bufoni zibanno!*' he cried.

In an instant, the Keelies were transformed into slimy toads, slinking about and burping dopily at Zorn's feet.

'There, now you have your own team of fly-catchers,' Mungo told him, before adding, 'And in your close company, there will surely be no shortage of flies for them to catch.'

Ignoring the general hilarity now being enjoyed at his expense, Zorn glanced at the toads, then looked directly at Mungo, a disdainful smirk on his lips. 'So, mighty Mungo,' he growled, 'the Master's chosen successor picks on little goblins. He demonstrates his powers with a puny trick that *I* could have bettered when but an infant.'

He snapped his fingers, and the toads immediately took the form of fully-grown lions, snarling, baring their teeth, pawing the air menacingly with their claws. Those near them shied swiftly away. Of a sudden, the sounds of communal merriment had been replaced by cries of alarm. Even the most able of sorcerers knew they would be no match for Zorn, if he chose to subject them to the unrestrained violence of his wrath.

Angered by Zorn's defiance, the Master quickly raised his staff and, aiming it at the lions, shouted, '*Leoni terminabbo!*'

In a burst of lightning, the lions reverted to being Keelies, who, unaware of their sudden return to goblin form, continued to roar and menace as if still kings of the jungle. The crowd started to laugh again, pointing at the Keelies' and aping their antics.

Zorn, meanwhile, swaggered slowly up to the throne and, with a contemptuous glance at Mungo, addressed the Master. 'So, old man, you fight your favourite's battles for him, huh? Well, we'll soon see what he's *really* worth!' He swiped the staff from the Master's hand and sent it rattling to the floor at Mungo's feet.

But before Mungo could reach down to retrieve it, a beam of green light from Zorn's eyes caused the staff to fly into his own hands. With everyone gaping in disbelief, he placed the centre of the staff over his raised knee.

'*This*,' he said to the Master as he snapped the sacred rod in two, 'is what I think of your precious little toy!'

Shouts of shocked disapproval rose from the body of the hall.

The Master was thunderstruck. 'You demented fool,' he snarled, ' – you have destroyed the hallowed symbol of our craft!'

Smirking derisively, Zorn hurled the broken staff to the floor. 'So!' he yelled at the Master. 'Where is it's Power now?' Turning then to Mungo, he bellowed, 'Your precious crutch is now firewood, and without its support you are nothing! *Nothing*!' Zorn's manic laughter echoed round the chamber, merging with a sudden low rumbling that steadily increased in volume while the castle began to shake.

An old warlock stepped out from the crowd and confronted Zorn. 'Sacrilege!' he cried. 'You have defiled the very soul of our ancient creed!' Those near him shouted their agreement, though alarm was beginning to spread throughout the hall as the rumbling grew louder and the tremors more violent.

'And now the Mighty One in the Higher Place is unleashing his wrath upon us all,' a haggard old witch hissed in Zorn's face. 'A curse upon your evil heart!'

'Do not threaten me, you feeble crone!' he barked, aiming a fiery bolt.

A cry of horror erupted from the onlooking crowd as, in a flash, the old woman was reduced to a molehill of smouldering ashes.

Zorn laughed manically again, looking up and around through crazed eyes, delighting in the damage that ever more violent shock waves were inflicting upon the castle. Large lumps of masonry and shattered roof timbers came crashing down on the masses inside the hall, and the more those suitably gifted tried to use their white magic to counter the devastation, the more Zorn drew on his mastery of the black arts to block them.

A state of panic was taking hold. Most guests not already maimed or killed were scattering, frantically seeking refuge from the deluge of debris now raining down. A few stood fast amid the billowing dust and offered up prayers to the Higher Place, begging the Mighty One for deliverance.

Yet Zorn showed nothing but cold-blooded indifference, becoming increasingly intoxicated by the pleasure he derived from being the instigator of such mayhem. And a drama unfolding by the throne was about to delight him even more.

Thrown off balance by the heaving floor, the Master had toppled over and had become trapped under a falling rafter. Mungo, clearly distraught, was preparing to utter a spell to raise the heavy beam from his beloved mentor's chest.

'No, please!' the old man wheezed, scarcely able to breathe. 'Please, conserve your strength to save yourself.'

'But, sire –' Mungo protested.

The Master weakly raised a hand. He shook his head, while the life blood began to drain from his wrinkled old cheeks. 'My time has come, my son.

My time … has come.'

'And so has yours, pipsqueak!' an angry voice yelled behind Mungo's back.

He wheeled round to see Zorn facing him, a murderous look in his eyes. But Mungo was undaunted. His hackles were up, his courage boosted by a sudden urge to avenge the agony that had been inflicted on the Master. 'You pit your strength not only against me, Zorn,' he shouted through the din of surrounding havoc, 'but also against that of the Mighty One, our great Lord who dwells all-seeing in the Higher Place.'

A belittling leer crossed Zorn's face. 'Your great Lord?' he scoffed. 'Ha! Look how he vents his anger on his quivering bootlickers!' He gestured vaguely towards those dead and dying souls who had come to witness Mungo's inauguration. 'Is this a mark of the *strength* of the Mighty One you kneel to?'

Young Mungo returned Zorn's stare, then stated calmly, 'It is the Mighty One's way.'

'Then I renounce your Mighty One!' Zorn screamed, his eyes glowing green with rage. 'For I, Zorn, serve a power much greater than his!'

A terrible roar filled the air as a gale swept through the castle. Thunder and lightning crashed and flashed all around. Zorn was staring wide-eyed upwards, laughing deliriously, his arms extended sideways, his hair swept back by the wind. Ghostly images of demons began to appear and disappear within the disintegrating hall: giant spectres, snarling, bellowing and clawing at their fleeing victims with razor-sharp talons.

Mungo looked at Zorn with undisguised disgust. 'The Prince of Darkness,' he muttered. 'You have sold your soul to *him*, haven't you?'

'YES!' Zorn boomed. He spun round to confront Mungo, his face contorted in a fiendish grin. 'And now it is *his* time to rule – through me. Through *ME-E-E-E*!'

Mungo's feelings of revulsion were now being overcome by a deep loathing for this once-respected wizard. Summoning up all his reserves of courage, he pointed his hand at Zorn, fingers spread, ready to release a bolt of energy. 'You and your evil overlord will never rule,' he growled through gritted teeth, '– not while I have breath in my body.'

'Which won't be for long!' Zorn countered. He grabbed Mungo's outstretched fingers and bent them back, forcing the young wizard to his knees. Then, with his free hand, he delivered a sickening blow to the side of Mungo's jaw. Blood oozed from Mungo's mouth as Zorn put a foot to his chest and, with one almighty shove, sent him sprawling over the floor. He landed on his back beside the Master, who appeared to have breathed his last. With tears filling his eyes, Mungo reached out and stroked the old man's hair. 'Master,' he whispered. 'Oh, my dearest Master...'

Zorn looked down at Mungo, revelling in the grief and humiliation he was subjecting him to. 'Why should I waste my magic powers in contest with the likes of you?' he mocked. 'Even in the crude fighting ways of mere mortals, you are no match for me!' He bent down and picked up a length of broken timber, then raised it like a club above Mungo's head. 'Now, you worthless weakling,' he barked, 'prepare to join your cherished Master in the so-called Higher Place!'

On the minstrel gallery, the Kiltie musicians were playing gamely on, in an effort to extend a measure of calm over the pandemonium raging below. But on seeing young Mungo's plight, one of the Kiltie pipers stopped playing, stepped to the front of the gallery and aimed the long drone of his bagpipes at Zorn. A scorching, needle-thin ray shot out and hit Zorn behind the ear, just as he was about to deliver the fatal blow to Mungo's head. Clasping his neck, Zorn dropped the piece of wood and glared up at the Kiltie band.

'Insolent vermin!' he yelled. 'You'll pay for that, you tone-deaf rat turds!'

This slight against their musicianship prompted two of the Kilties to leap down, latch onto Zorn's drooping moustache and start kicking him about the chest. While Zorn was grappling with this pair, the Kiltie marksman on the gallery drew a bead on a carefully-selected target and fired another searing ray from his bagpipes. This time, the shot hit Zorn squarely where every Kiltie wears his sporran. Groaning in agony, and with smoke rising from the front of his breeches, Zorn dropped to his knees, bent double, his eyes watering.

Floods of unbridled giggling cascaded down from the other musicians.

Though still feeling groggy from the blow to his jaw, young Mungo saw his chance. He clambered to his feet and, before Zorn could defend himself, kicked him full in the face.

Now it was Zorn's turn to spit blood, though his fury became even more intense. He had never in all the centuries allowed his bullying ways to be defied by those he regarded as lesser beings, and he had no intention of letting such audacity go unpunished now. Shrugging off the pain inflicted by their bagpiping comrade, he took hold of the two Kilties swinging from his moustache and threw them aside as if they were rag dolls.

'So, *magnificent* Mungo,' he growled, 'first that spent old wizard and now these puny little gremlins had to come to your aid, eh? Well,' he smirked, 'we'll see about that!' He pointed up at the minstrel gallery and released a flash of lightning that hurled the Kiltie musicians with bone-shattering force against the crumbling stone wall behind them.

'You cold-blooded murderer!' Mungo growled. 'Anyone capable of such a cowardly act isn't even fit to breathe the same air as the old Master, far less take his place.'

Zorn gave a defiant laugh, then looked around in delight at the ongoing destruction of the castle.

Mungo was quivering with rage now. All the pent-up feelings of being inferior to this heartless bully suddenly boiled into a potent brew of hatred and vengeance. All the values of love and forgiveness that he'd learned to respect during his long years of training in the Brotherhood suddenly became irrelevant. Slowly, he raised his hand and took aim. 'May the Mighty One forgive me for what I am about to do,' he said under his breath, then directed a thunderbolt at Zorn's head. 'Die, you evil maniac!' he barked. '*Die!*'

But Zorn merely smiled smugly and, with little apparent effort, deflected the blazing shaft of light with the palm of his hand. 'Your best is not good enough,' he laughed, taunting Mungo to continue his attack, while relishing the sight of his young adversary becoming exhausted in the process. Gathering his brows into a scowl, he pointed a forefinger at Mungo. '*DEBOLEO APAGABBO!*' he shouted. A rod of lightning thudded into Mungo's chest, propelling him backwards onto the floor, where he lay struggling for breath.

Zorn ambled forward and stood over him, ready for the kill. 'And you thought you were fit to be the new Master, did you?' He answered his own question with a burst of manic laughter. '*I*, Zorn,' he yelled, 'am the new Master, and you are nothing – *nothing*!'

'May you rot in hell!' Mungo gasped.

Zorn fixed him in a malicious stare. '*This* is hell now. And *I* will rule over it, while you rot beneath the rubble of your *Mighty* One's great house!'

Mungo glanced at the scenes of utter devastation all around: fires burning among the fallen masonry, the dead and injured strewn everywhere. 'A curse on your treacherous soul!' he hissed.

'I spit on your puny curse,' Zorn snarled, then pinned Mungo's head to the floor with his foot. 'The Power is mine! *MINE*!' He raised his eyes skyward, hands outstretched in mock adulation. 'Prepare, Oh Mighty One, to welcome your vanquished disciple!' he roared, before dissolving once more into fits of crazed laughter.

Then, chillingly, he fell silent. Breathing hard, he glared down at his helpless prey, pressing the side of his head into the rubble-strewn floor with his foot. Hatred was burning in his eyes as he slowly and deliberately aimed the spread fingers of both hands at Mungo's body. 'And now *you* will die, slowly, like a cringing dog, beneath the heel of your true Master.'

'*DEBOLEO MORABBO!*' he yelled. With rays of fire flashing from his fingers, he stared in delight at Mungo writhing in pain as flames licked hungrily over his body.

In a frantic bid to survive, Mungo dredged up the last traces of his strength. Pointing a shaking hand at Zorn, he released a bolt of lightning, only to see it deflected with a derisory flick of the wrist.

As futile as Mungo's effort had been, the will to live that it showed was enough to drive Zorn into an even more vicious rage. With a roar, he redoubled the ferocity of his attack, propelling Mungo's body into convulsions of agony.

But strangely, just as he felt consciousness fading away, Mungo sensed the deadly energy that was torturing him begin to subside. He was given yet another straw of hope to clutch as the weight of Zorn's foot was removed from his head. Blinking away the tears of pain, he could see Zorn staggering back, clasping his throat, choking. Mungo rubbed his eyes and turned his head towards a moaning sound coming from somewhere on the floor close by. There he saw the Master, still trapped beneath the heavy wooden beam. Though clearly at death's door, the old wizard was conscious and doggedly holding together the two pieces of his broken staff. From its tip, a shaft of intense light was searing into Zorn's chest.

The Master's voice was frail and unsteady, but no less commanding for that. 'I am bound by the ancient laws of the Brotherhood,' he declared, 'to condemn you, Zorn, to languish in the bowels of the earth – for ever!'

A deafening thunderclap rent the air, and the earth shook as a ragged cleft began to open at Zorn's feet. He could not hide his fury, nor conceal his desperation to avoid the awful fate that now awaited him. Yet he realised that escape was impossible, for there could be no resistance to the Power of the sacred staff, now restored. A doomed man, Zorn teetered on the edge of the widening crevice, from which flames and clouds of sulphurous smoke were now belching.

'*NO-O-O!*' he howled, the sound of his voice resembling the frantic bellowing of an animal caught in a trap.

The Master observed this vain show of defiance with a blend of revulsion and pity. But though his supernatural energies were now all but drained, the old High Sorcerer knew that his work in this world was not quite over. Struggling to find the strength, he pointed his staff at Zorn. 'With my last breath,' he gasped, 'I now commit you for all time to the infernal depths of hell!'

Yet, no matter how hopeless his situation, Zorn was determined not to be vanquished without leaving his mark. With a final, desperate lunge, he reached out and snatched one half of the sacred staff from the Master's hand, before being sucked over the edge of the flaming chasm, yelling oaths of vengeance as he went.

Mungo looked in anguish towards the Master, hoping against hope that he might yet live on, that the Mighty One might yet delay calling him to the Higher Place. But it was not to be. The old man, his last act of goodness done, slumped lifeless on the floor of what remained of Goblin Hall Castle, while Zorn descended into the fiery abyss to which he had been condemned.

'In the name of my Lord Lucifer,' he roared back at Mungo, 'I swear I will take my revenge for this – even if I have to wait until hell itself freezes over!'

* * * * *

− CHAPTER SIX −

THE PRESENT DAY − OUTSIDE OLD MUNGO'S COTTAGE...

'And that was how the great castle of Goblin Hall was destroyed,' Mungo told the children in conclusion of his tale.

'What a shame,' said Susie. 'What a terrible shame.'

'Ah, yes − a terrible shame indeed,' old Mungo agreed. 'But good triumphed over bad, so such a price was justified, you see.'

Something was still troubling Jamie, though. 'What about the Kilties?' he asked.

'That's right,' said Susie. 'What about the Kilties? They were good goblins, but some of them still got zapped by Zorn, and he was a baddie.'

'*Is* a baddie,' old Mungo corrected. Then, not wishing to have that unsavoury detail gone into further, he added, 'But don't you go worrying about the Kilties. Plenty survived, and they're still around, never fear.'

'Well, *I've* never seen one,' said Jamie.

Mungo patted his head. 'Hmm, but you will ... if you believe.'

'And what about the magic stick?' Susie wanted to know.

'The Master's staff?' Mungo reached inside a fold of his robe. 'This is one part of it. I am duty bound to keep it with me for ever, but without the other half...'

'Yes,' Susie chipped in, 'and Zorn pinched that, didn't he?'.

'Pinched my mouse too,' Jamie mumbled, still pained by the thought. 'Pinched Jasper.'

Mungo nodded ruefully, but decided to continue sidestepping that touchy topic.

A few moments of thoughtful silence passed before Susie said hesitantly, 'Ehm, Mungo...?'

'Uh-huh?'

'Why can't you do *real* magic any more?'

'Oh, I lack the Power,' Mungo sighed. 'Simple as that. Yes, that big confrontation with Zorn all those centuries ago drained most of it, I'm afraid.'

Jamie pointed to the hill with the dead tree on top. 'What about that?'

'That's right,' Susie said, 'you could fill up at the old tree, couldn't you?'

Mungo allowed himself a quiet chuckle. 'Ah well, I's not quite as simple as that, you see. No, not like taking your coach to a petrol pump or something like that, in this day and age. Oh my, no, no, no.'

'Why not?' Jamie asked in that no-beating-about-the-bush way that comes naturally to a five-year-old.

Mungo was caught on the back foot. 'Eh – uh – *why*?'

'Yes, why?' Susie and Jamie said together.

'Well, it – it's because...' Mungo was getting into a tizzy. 'Well, you might not understand. I mean, it's a bit complicated, a mite difficult to explain to little –'

'Why?' the children persisted, their eyes never leaving Mungo's face.

'It – it's because … well, because it's a bit like, uhm, let me see…' Mungo scratched his head. 'Yes, that's it – it's a bit like charging a battery, you might say, in this day and age, so to speak.' He looked hopefully at the children over the top of his specs. 'Do you see what I mean?'

Susie and Jamie shook their heads.

Old Mungo stroked his chin, thinking hard. 'Right,' he said at length, 'let me put it this way…'

* * *

CANTRIP COTTAGE – LATER THE SAME DAY...

Maggie had done a lot of work since the removal men left in the morning. Admittedly, there was still much more to do before the cottage would resemble the cosy little home she envisaged. But at least the bulk of the furniture was in place, and *some* of the seemingly endless piles of cardboard boxes had been emptied. She'd even found time to hang a few pictures on the walls, and the log fire was burning cheerily in the old black grate in the living room – much to Charlie the dog's approval. Maggie emerged from the kitchen carrying two plates of baked beans on toast, which she placed in front of Susie and Jamie on the table by the window, from where they could see the hilltop with the outline of its dead tree etched against the evening sky.

'And that's what happened to the castle,' said Susie. 'Honest, Mum.'

Magie responded with an understanding though weary little smile. 'Yes, yes, I'm sure it was. Now, eat up. It'll soon be bedtime.'

'Aw, Mum…' Susie and Jamie protested.

Maggie knelt down in the middle of the floor with her back to the children and began to lift some books out of a cardboard box. 'Well, I did tell you to come straight home from old Mungo's. It's your own fault you're late for supper.'

'That's right,' Susie eagerly agreed, before stuffing a forkful of beans into her mouth. 'A-and old Mungo … he told us all about the old dead tree out there and *every*thing!'

'Don't speak with your mouth full, dear,' Maggie muttered, leafing through a book.

'Yeah, the Frightening Tree,' Jamie piped up, his imagination still fired by Mungo's tale.

'It's the *Light*ning Tree,' Susie corrected in her big-sisterly way.

'Never mind,' said Maggie absently. 'Just eat up, hmm.'

'Yes,' Susie replied to the back of her mother's head, 'but when he – I mean old Mungo – when he stands under the dead tree like he does, that's him charging up his magic power.'

But Maggie wasn't really listening. 'Mmm, I'm sure … I'm sure.'

The children busied themselves with the task of tucking into their supper for a couple of minutes, then Susie spoke to her mother again: 'He hasn't got much left, though.'

'Hmm? Much what?'

'Batteries,' said Jamie.

'Honestly, Jamie!' Maggie chuckled, then laid down the book and lifted another from the box. 'Batteries, indeed...'

But Jamie was undeterred. 'Needs the lightning, see?'

The little boy and his sister then gazed out of the window at the old dead tree.

'Mungo says he can only plug into the Lightning Tree once in his whole life, Mum,' said Susie in the most serious of tones.

Jamie nodded his agreement. 'Well, for the really *big* power anyway,' he added after a thoughtful pause.

Susie glared at him and put a finger to her lips. 'Sh-h-h-h! We promised!'

They returned to the business of eating their beans on toast, while making secretive faces to one another behind their mother's back.

'Yes, I'm going to have a word with your Mr Mungo,' Maggie said. 'I'll tell him to stop putting such silly ideas into your heads.' She laid down her book, then turned to face the children, a reproachful look on her face. 'Flying piglets, Lightning Trees, bagpipes firing laser beams centuries before lasers were even dreamed about? Honestly, I've never heard such nonsense.'

Susie and Jamie glanced at each other, but remained silent.

Maggie got up and walked over to their table. 'Anyway, that was your Gran on the phone this afternoon. She's sending Grandpa over to pick you up first thing in the morning. You'll be spending a couple of days with them while I finish off here.' She looked about the room. 'Phew! Still *loads* to do!'

The expression on Jamie's face made it plain that he wasn't at all keen on this latest development.

The look wasn't lost on his mother. 'Well?' she probed.

Jamie lowered his eyes. 'Can't go.'

Maggie tweaked his cheek. 'Of course you can. You'll have great fun, like always.'

Jamie shook his head while staring glumly at his plate. 'Got to stay here and save Jasper.'

Maggie bent down and gave him a hug. 'Honestly, you and that mouse of yours. You're always losing him. Come on, cheer up. I'll probably find him in the laundry basket … among your smelly socks as usual, right?'

But Jamie's expression only became more solemn. He continued to shake his head, on the verge of tears.

Maggie watched him, a lump rising in her throat. Yet, even if it seemed harsh, she had no option but to take a more practical view of the Jasper situation than her little boy. 'Oh, Jamie,' she murmured, laying her hand on his head, 'he'll turn up, never you fear.'

Susie had been observing all of this very closely, and her sympathies lay with Jamie. She gave her mother an old-fashioned look and addressed her as if their ages had suddenly become reversed. 'I don't think,' she said quietly but firmly, 'that you fully understand the bond that exists between a boy and his mouse, do you, Mother?'

Maggie lifted her shoulders in a great, shuddering sigh. What, after all, could a grown woman say to counter such a profound observation from her own seven-year-old daughter?

* * * * *

– CHAPTER SEVEN –

TROWIE GLEN –
AFTER DARK THAT SAME NIGHT...

Old Mungo was sitting alone outside the front door of his cottage, leaning forward in his rocking chair, resting his chin on clasped hands. He was gazing over the valley towards the ruins of Goblin Hall Castle, the jagged remains of its walls silhouetted against a rising moon. 'What a shame,' he murmured wistfully.

Just then, Jake the jackdaw fluttered out of the darkness and landed on his shoulder. '*What a shame*,' he cawed.

Mungo nodded his head. 'Hmm, what a shame, Jake. What a terrible shame...'

Up at Cantrip Cottage, meanwhile, Susie and Jamie had been asleep for hours, though Maggie had only just gone to bed. She looked towards her bedside table, on which she had placed a framed photograph of a handsome young man in his thirties. 'Good night,' she whispered, then switched off the light and laid her head on the pillow, smiling sadly, tears trickling down her cheeks. 'Good night ... Jim.'

Though her heart was still heavy, Maggie realised the only way to face life now was to count her blessings, to be thankful for the wonderful times she'd shared with Jim, and look forward to creating a new life for herself and their children. Nothing would ever be the same, of course, but it was comforting to know that Susie and Jamie were coping well, all things considered – not least making the acquaintance of a certain dotty old man! But she was sure Mungo was harmless enough, and the children would soon find things more worthwhile than daft stories about bagpiping goblins and battling wizards to occupy their minds. Maggie snuggled down to try and get some much-needed sleep, thinking thoughts of happy times past and, she hoped, happy times to come again … one day.

*

AN HOUR OR SO LATER...

Although the cottage was small, it had three bedrooms, so, as in their previous house, Susie and Jamie had been allotted one each. Charlie the dog had long been in the habit of sleeping in whichever of the children's rooms happened to take his fancy. On this occasion, he had chosen to grace Susie with his company, and was curled up asleep at the foot of her bed. Suddenly, he raised his head, ears pricked. Looking towards the door, he gave a low growl. The moon was already high, its light streaming through the window and casting unfamiliar shadows across the room. Charlie's eyes were fixed on the door handle, which started to turn, ever so slowly. The little dog swiftly sought refuge on Susie's pillow, nudging her teddy bear from the crook of her arm as he attempted to burrow beneath the covers.

Susie opened one drowsy eye. 'Charlie!' she snapped. 'Bad dog! You'll make Teddy angry!'

Then the door creaked. In an instant, Susie was wide awake. She caught her breath, watching pop-eyed as the door opened, inch by inch, and a small, shadowy figure crept silently into the room. Susie sat up, terrified. 'A Keelie!' she gulped, and clutched Teddy tightly.

Charlie promptly crawled under the duvet and made for the foot of the bed.

As the intruder moved closer and closer, Susie tried to scream, but all that came out was a puny little squawk. She made a desperate effort to reach out and bang on the wall between her room and her mother's, but only succeeded in falling out of bed. Beside herself with fear, she looked up to see a face staring down at her. Even in the pale light of the moon, she could make out the features. And she knew them well.

'Jamie!' she gasped. 'What are *you* doing up? It's still night time! And – and – and you gave – you gave *Charlie* an awful fright!'

She could see that her little brother had managed to dress himself, and although he'd made a bit of a hash of it, he was clearly in no mind to go back to bed.

He pointed glumly at his trainers. 'Will you tie them for me, Susie?'

Brushing aside all evidence of her recent attack of helplessness, Susie resumed an air of big-sisterly superiority. 'Really, Jamie,' she scolded, 'you're *so* useless at times!'

That went in one of Jamie's ears and straight out the other. He indicated the laces of his trainers again. 'Will you tie them for me, Susie … *please*?' He paused to look her in the eye, then added, 'I'm going for Jasper!'

Susie inhaled slowly and deeply, that old-fashioned expression on her face again. She told herself that someone like her, a young lady of seven (well, seven-and-a-quarter to be exact) with so much more experience of life than a mere five-year-old – and a five-year-old *boy* to boot – should really be doing all she could to discourage such a rash idea. But then again, she *did* understand the bond that exists between a boy and his mouse, so she tied Jamie's laces and proceeded to get dressed herself.

Ten minutes later, the back door of the cottage eased open and Charlie crept out, snarling at the moon. Susie, torch in hand, appeared next, with Jamie close behind. A dog howled somewhere in the darkness of the glen, adding another measure of scariness to an already scary scene. Charlie retreated behind the children's legs, whining.

'Sh-h-h-h, Charlie!' Susie hissed. 'You'll wake Mum up!'

Upstairs in her bedroom, Maggie had stirred at the sound of the dog howling, but quickly turned over and tried to go back to sleep. After all, in any new neighbourhood there were bound to be lots of new noises to get used to. The main thing was that the children were safely tucked up in bed, sound asleep and none the worse for their 'adventures' of the previous day. Or so she thought...

Holding hands, Susie and Jamie stepped into the darkness, peering nervously about. Charlie followed in their footsteps, uttering jittery little growls at noises only he could hear. At the bottom of the valley, something large and white rose flapping from the parapet of a little bridge they were approaching. They ducked as the apparition swooped past their heads.

'*EE-EE-EE-K*!' Susie screamed.

'*WA-A-A-AH*!' Jamie yelled. 'That a ghost?'

'D-don't *think* so,' Susie stammered, hopefully.

The sound of an owl hooting drifted away into the gloom.

'Was *def*in'ly a ghost!' Jamie declared.

Charlie trembled, as did both children.

'You scared, Jamie?'

'No... d-don't *think* so.'

'M-me too.'

They crossed the bridge, step by cautious step, and entered the woods on the other side. Up ahead, the moonlit turrets of the castle could now be seen towering above the treetops. A breath of wind whispered through the trees, stirring their branches and setting spidery shadows scuttling over the ground. Susie and Jamie almost jumped out of their skins as a hollow tree suddenly loomed out of the darkness in their path, its gnarled branches clawing the sky like the fingers of a witch. More scared than ever now, they hurried past, not daring to look back.

For minutes that seemed like hours, they stumbled on through jaggy undergrowth and squelchy puddles, before entering a clearing, where at last their goal appeared before them. As a cloud drifted over the face of the moon, Susie and Jamie stood staring up at the ruins of Goblin Hall Castle: grim and menacing, yet majestic too – in a spooky sort of way.

Unseen by the children, green-glowing eyes were looking at them from the cover of the surrounding woods. Two Keelie goblins were watching their every move. One of them let out a sinister chuckle.

Susie spun round. 'What was that?'

Jamie shook his head. He didn't know, and preferred not think about it anyway.

The Keelies exchanged scheming glances, then made for the shadows of the castle. Only Charlie could hear the rustle of their feet wading through the carpet of dead leaves. He growled, nervously.

'Quiet, Charlie!' said Susie in a gruff whisper. 'You're giving me the creeps!'

Inside the castle, the two Keelies shuffled into what had once been the great hall, its roof now open to the sky, its floor strewn with rubble. While one Keelie grunted in anticipation, the other pointed a finger at a large stone slab standing four-square against one wall.

'*Adzapp*!' he rasped. '*Adzapp aperto*!'

There was a grating crunch as the slab began to slide slowly aside, revealing a narrow stairway that led down through the floor. The Keelies looked over their shoulders to make sure they hadn't been noticed. Then, with the 'door' left open behind them, they scampered down the stairs, sniggering in delight.

Back outside, Susie and Jamie stepped warily across the clearing, gazing up in awe as they came closer to the castle. Without warning, a strong wind rose up, sending clouds scudding across the sky, and making the woods moan and groan as if possessed by demons. Of a sudden, the echo of a man's laughter, evil-sounding laughter, mingled with the wailing of the wind. The children stopped in their tracks, startled and confused, their eyes darting from side to side.

* * *

IN ZORN'S UNDERGROUND LAIR...

Slime oozed from the walls of this cavernous chamber, in which dripping stalactites hung from the ceiling like grotesque stone icicles. A dim green light lent an eeriness to the place, and spurts of flame shot up from clefts in the floor, polluting the air with billows of smoke and the stench of rotten eggs.

From the mouth of a tunnel, huddles of scraggy figures, their bodies clad in sackcloth, were hauling wagons heaped with coal. While Keelies lashed them with whips, these wretched creatures shovelled their loads into a pit on the opposite side of the cave, before being herded back to begin their cycle of torture all over again.

The same evil-sounding laughter that had startled the children a few moments earlier rang out again – though louder now and nearer. Much nearer...

Zorn, still in the garb of a Viking warrior, but with his head bared to reveal stubby horns sprouting from his skull, was reclining on a stone throne overlooking this hellish scene. Talking excitedly to him were Scurvo and Tentor, the two Keelies who had been watching the children from the cover of the woods. They were looking extremely pleased with themselves.

'So, my cunning little minions,' Zorn beamed, 'part-one of my plan works, does it?'

'Yes, yes, yes, indeed,' Scurvo giggled. Tentor nodded his head as rapidly as a woodpecker hammering on a tree trunk. 'It is true, oh Great One – the mortal brats are coming.'

'Brilliant!' said Zorn. He reached down and produced a tiny cage from the side of his throne. Cowering in a corner was Jasper. Zorn laughed manically and punched the air. '*YES*! Brilliant *is* the word! For who but *I* could set a mouse to catch a wizard?'

* * *

BACK IN THE WOODLAND CLEARING...

Zorn's crazed laughter rose again on the wind, then faded into the night.

Susie tugged Jamie's sleeve. 'M-maybe we should go home.'

'No!' her little brother scowled. 'Not going without Jasper!'

Although Susie knew that turning back was the only sensible thing to do, she was far too frightened to go on her own. So, with Jamie now leading the way, they edged ever closer to the castle. But then something stirred just ahead. Unknown to them, it was another Keelie, loitering in the shadows, watching. It skulked out of sight the moment Susie flashed her torch in its direction. The children stood frozen to the spot, listening.

'Maybe just a rabbit?' Susie suggested, optimistically.

Jamie didn't know, so once again decided the best thing to do was pretend nothing had happened. He tightened his grip on his big sister's hand. 'Come on, Susie! Nearly there!'

A few moments later, the children, with Charlie still in close attendance, were stepping hesitantly through the vast arched entrance of the castle, gazing upwards and around at the spooky scene. By the time they'd arrived within the walls of the great hall, the moaning of the wind could no longer be heard. But silence only added to the creepiness of the place.

'Oo-oo-oo!' Susie quavered. 'I hope it isn't haunted in here!'

'Haunted?' said Jamie. 'What does that word mean?'

Fortunately for him, Susie could scarcely bear to think about it, far less try to explain. But she feared the castle was about to reveal the awful truth anyway, when behind them something crashed to the floor. Charlie yapped hysterically as several large bats swept out of the darkness and fluttered past, screeching. One brushed against Susie's face.

'*YEE-EE-EE-EEP*!' she screamed. '*Vampires*!'

'*WHOO-OO-OO-OO*!' Jamie bawled. '*Van-pies*!'

A quivery, rattling noise rose from where the mysterious 'thing' had clattered down.

'S-sounds like a skeleton!' Susie warbled.

'Don't know what a skelingtin is,' Jamie muttered. Then, true to the belief that ignorance is bliss, he turned and took a step in the direction of the noise, making a commendable show of fearlessness, but keeping a firm grip on his sister's hand all the same. He pointed towards the way they'd come in. 'Make the torch shine over there, Susie. I think that's where the skelingtin landed.'

Susie did as instructed, while crouching down behind her little brother and peeping wide-eyed over his shoulder. Charlie had already taken cover behind Susie's legs.

'Stop shaking the torch,' Jamie grouched. 'It's making me seasick!'

Susie's reply came in the form of a weepy yodel. 'N-not my fault. It–it–it's my knees. Can you not hear them knocking?'

'Just thought it was the skelingtin.'

Susie was too busy holding back the tears to be bothered responding to such a silly remark. But when the beam from her torch finally found its target, it revealed nothing more frightening than an old sheet of plywood, which had been blown by the wind and lay flapping on a pile of rubble. For all that, the children were now in such a state of jumpiness that even Jamie was having second thoughts about continuing their quest to rescue Jasper. Surprisingly though, it would turn out to be Charlie he'd have to thank for bolstering his determination to carry on – albeit in a roundabout sort of way...

While the children were trying to calm their nerves, something else in the dark interior of the ruins caught the little dog's attention. He gave one of his low growls.

'Stop it, Charlie!' Susie said sharply. 'There's nothing there!'

Jamie wasn't so sure. 'M-maybe that rabbit again?'

Susie gripped his arm, tightly. 'Hmm ... prob'ly.'

Charlie was staring towards whatever he'd heard – or seen. He snarled, his ruff rising, then started to bark, the sound reverberating round the crumbling old walls.

Although his heart was racing, Jamie bent down and gave his little pal a pat on the head. 'It's all right, Charlie. Don't be fright'ed. I – I'll look after you...'

Whether it was Jamie's reassurance or a harking-back to distant wolf-like forebears that gave Charlie's boldness a boost is neither here nor there; whatever the reason, he took off and bounded out of sight behind a heap of fallen masonry. There, he came face-to-face with the Keelie, who glared at him through angry green eyes. Charlie inched closer, threatening, baring his teeth.

But this was only playing into the Keelie's hands.

He snapped his fingers and transformed himself into a huge brown rat. While Charlie gaped in bewilderment, the rat crouched down, hissing menacingly, then darted past him.

Susie noticed the slinky shape scurrying through the shadows. '*EE-EE-EEK*!' she squealed. '*A rat*!'

With Charlie in hot pursuit, the Keelie-rat made a dash for the opening in the wall that the other two Keelies had slunk into earlier. It raced through and promptly disappeared into the darkness of the stairway.

'Charlie!' Jamie yelled. 'Don't go there, Charlie! COME BACK!'

Too late. Charlie had already gone.

Susie started to sob. 'Oh, Charlie,' she sniffled. 'We'll never see you again … *ever*.'

But Jamie was made of sterner stuff. He gestured towards the opening in the wall. 'I bet that's where the bad man that took Jasper lives.' He put a hand on his sister's back and gave her a shove. 'Come on, Susie. We're going in!'

* * * * *

– CHAPTER EIGHT –

THE SUBTERRANEAN PASSAGEWAY TO ZORN'S CAVERN

Charlie, still barking gamely, was chasing the rat through a dark, cobweb-draped tunnel that had bats hanging from the ceiling like clusters of wet rags, and air that was thick with the smell of rotting fungus. Suddenly, the rat turned and stood its ground. Charlie stopped in his tracks, growling, but wary. In the blink of an eye, the rat changed back into a Keelie and began mocking the little dog by aping a matador taunting a bull with his cape.

Out of the shadows, four more Keelies emerged. They had a net stretched out in front of them. Charlie tried to make a break for it in the opposite direction, only to have his way blocked by yet more Keelies. Panic-stricken, the little dog looked desperately for another way to escape, but there was nothing he could do but stand and whimper as the pack of evil goblins closed in.

Deep underground, Zorn was sitting on his throne, with Scurvo and Tentor, his principal Keelie sidekicks, still in attendance. They were watching a giant, cloud-like 'screen', which was hovering high above the floor of the cave. Projected on it were live pictures of Charlie, yelping in terror as the Keelie gang's nets were flung over him. Zorn smiled a twisted smile. He nodded his head, and the scene on the cloud switched to the great hall of the castle, where Susie and Jamie could be seen approaching the opening in the wall.

Zorn rubbed his hands. '*Yes*!' he smirked. 'The bait for my trap will soon be in place!'

* * *

BACK INSIDE THE GREAT HALL...

The children stepped cautiously through the stone doorway. Susie shivered as she shone her torch into the darkness. 'Oo-oo-oo, it's creepy in here, Jamie! M-maybe we should go and get Mummy to come with us.'

Jamie was just as scared as his sister, but determined not to show it. Summoning up every ounce of his courage, he took a firm grip of her hand and led her towards the stairs. Just as they were about to take the first downward step, there was a shrill squawk, then a black shape materialised out of nowhere and landed on Susie's head.

'*WA-A-A-AH*!' yelled Jamie. 'Another van-pie!'

Susie let out a blood-curdling screech and promptly dropped the torch. She raised her hands to her ears, but couldn't bear to touch the thing on her head. 'Help, Jamie! It's a bat! A *bat* – in my *hair*!'

From what old Effie the housekeeper had told them, Jamie knew well enough what the horrible consequences of this would be. Without wasting a second, he got down on his knees and started to fumble about in the darkness. Susie, petrified, continued to scream.

'Got it!' Jamie shouted as his fingers finally made contact with the torch. 'Don't be fright'ed any more, Susie. I, uh – I just need to find a pair of scissors next!'

This well-meaning but somewhat ill-considered statement only succeeded in making Susie feel even more destitute. 'I want Mummy,' she wailed. 'I want Mummy – *now*!'

His hands shaking, Jamie moved the beam of the torch upwards from Susie's feet, dreading what he'd discover when it reached her hair. The last thing he expected, though, was to hear a croaky cry of:

'*Silly bugger, Jake*!'

Jamie was so relieved to see old Mungo's jackdaw perched on his sister's head that he started to giggle.

But Susie was in no mood for jollity. She was crying uncontrollably now. '*Off*! Get it *off* me, Jamie!'

Although he wasn't exactly *scared* of Jake, Jamie wasn't all that keen on getting too close to him either. He remembered something else old Effie had told them – a song she sometimes sang – about two Scottish crows – 'corbies' or something she called them – and they found a dead man lying behind a wall. A knight it was – a knight with shiny armpits or something – and the crows were going to poke his eyes out for their dinner. Yes, and Jamie was sure Jake was some kind of crow as well, with a sharp beak and everything.

He tried shouting '*Shoo*!' a few times, but Jake paid no heed. So, very cagily, Jamie extended his hand towards Susie's head. 'Here, birdie,' he said, closing his eyes tightly. 'Come to me, birdie ... *please.*'

Jake obediently hopped down onto the little boy's wrist.

'I *hate* that silly bird,' Susie blubbered. She rubbed the top of her head, though it was probably her pride that had been hurt more than anything.

It was then that Jamie noticed Jake was holding something in his beak: two gold coins, which he promptly dropped into Jamie's hand.

'*Magic money*! *Magic money*!' croaked Jake, then flew off as swiftly as he'd appeared.

Jamie stared at the coins, intrigued, then stuck a finger up his nostril. 'The nose pennies,' he muttered, recalling the magic trick that Jake had performed for them outside old Mungo's cottage the previous day. But he was rudely jolted back to the present by the sound of a dog yelping somewhere deep underground. He grabbed his sister's hand again. 'Come on, Susie. Charlie's in trouble!'

'But I'm scared, Jamie. I mean, I *really* think we should go and get Mummy.'

'No time! Charlie needs us!'

Susie was about to object again when a harsh, scraping noise came from behind them. The children turned to see the stone 'door' they had just come through slide shut. Horror-struck, they started to thump on it with their hands, shouting at the top of the voices. But to no avail.

'It's no good,' Susie sobbed as she finally slumped exhausted against the cold stone. 'Nobody can hear us.'

Although Jamie was now on the verge of tears himself, he tried to console his sister by telling her not to worry; he would look after her. But, as before, Jamie's well-intentioned words only added to Susie's sense of despair.

Just then, the sound of a dog yelping rose up again from somewhere far below.

Jamie nudged Susie's arm. 'Listen – they're hurting Charlie! Come on!'

Susie looked at the wall of rock that imprisoned them, then at the dark void of the stairs. She felt utterly helpless, yet didn't want to let herself down *completely* in front of her little brother. After all, she was the one who'd boasted about understanding the bond that exists between a boy and his mouse, so she only had herself to blame for being in this mess now. She wiped her nose on her sleeve, sniffed, and squared her shoulders. 'All right,' she said, 'I'll go with you.' Then, readopting an air of big-sisterly authority, she held out her hand. 'But *I*'ll take the torch, if you don't mind!'

* * *

BACK AT CANTRIP COTTAGE, MEANWHILE...

Maggie had been sleeping fitfully, tossing and turning in her bed, unable to clear her mind of all the things she would have to do before the cottage became the home she wanted for the children. Suddenly, she sat up, fully awake.

'What was that?' she called out. 'Susie? ... Did you just shout? ... Susie? ... Jamie?'

But all she could hear was an owl hooting somewhere on the other side of the glen. She told herself she must have been dreaming. After all, the children were safely tucked up in bed, and if they'd wanted her, they'd have come through to her room. Still, better make sure, just in case one of them was having a nightmare, which wouldn't be surprising, considering all the scary goblin-and-wizard nonsense old Mungo had been filling their heads with. Maggie got out of bed and tiptoed along the corridor to Susie's room first. She opened the door, ever so quietly, and peeped inside. But Susie's bed was empty. Not to worry, thought Maggie — she'd most likely be in Jamie's room, keeping him company. That did happen occasionally, if he'd wakened up and couldn't get back to sleep. And now that she thought about it, maybe she shouldn't have given them those baked beans for supper. Jamie *had* been known to wake himself up by farting in bed. She slipped along to his room and, once again, poked her head round the door without making a sound.

Seconds later, Maggie was downstairs, switching on lights and rushing from room to room. But the children were nowhere to be seen. And no Charlie the dog either. Then she noticed a piece of paper on the kitchen table. On it was scrawled a short message:

'*GON FOR JASPA – SUSIE.*'

Maggie raised a hand to her lips. What on earth did Susie mean? She stood for a moment, trying to think clearly, willing herself not to panic. 'Jasper...' she murmured. 'Old Mungo... I wonder...' She rushed back upstairs and threw on some clothes.

The rosy glow of dawn was just beginning to spread along the skyline as Maggie ran stumbling down the glen to old Mungo's cottage. She started to bang loudly on the front door, but there was no response. Already frantic with worry, she was now almost weeping with frustration as well. 'Come on! Come *on*!' she growled. 'Answer the *door*, will you!'

Maggie gave a little gasp as she felt a hand touch her shoulder. She wheeled round to see old Mungo standing there, dressed in the same long robe as before.

'Mistress McKim,' he said, smiling sweetly. 'My apologies. I'm afraid I startled you.'

'Yes... No... That is, I – I thought you must have been in bed – asleep.'

Mungo's smile broadened, and he shook his head. 'Hmm, no need for sleep ... at my age.'

Maggie had neither the time nor inclination to ask what he meant by that. 'The point is,' she said, 'I'm looking for...' She handed him Susie's note. '...my daughter, she left this. I – I thought that maybe you...'

Mungo's expression grew more solemn as he read the little girl's message. 'Mmm,' he nodded, 'just as I feared.'

'*Feared*'? What do you mean, feared?'

Mungo returned the note, then gazed over the glen towards the ruined castle of Goblin Hall, it's ghostly outline just visible through the trees above a blanket of mist. 'I told them not to go near that place.'

'*Place*? What place?

'Zorn,' said Mungo, as if to himself. 'I fear he had it planned all along.'

Maggie was almost at her wits' end. 'Zorn? Planned? I don't understand. What – what are you *saying*, for heaven's sake?'

Mungo looked at Maggie, his expression remorseful now. 'The fault is all mine, Mistress McKim. I tried to make the boy's mouse fly. Oh yes, a simple enough task, you might say, but ... well, it's been so long, and I just –'

'Make his mouse fly?' Maggie scowled. 'A mouse *fly*?' She could scarcely believe what she was hearing. 'What *is* all this nonsense?' Without waiting for a reply, she turned to leave. 'I'm going to phone the police!'

Mungo laid a hand on her arm. 'Please, Mistress McKim, if you want to see your children again, you must do as I say.'

As Maggie tried to pull away, Mungo's fingers closed. 'Please, you have to believe me. This is now between Zorn and me.'

'Zorn? I don't know what you're –'

'I must go to the Lightning Tree,' Mungo interrupted. 'And without a moment's delay!'

Maggie was becoming more anxious about the children every time this old oddball spoke. 'No!'

she insisted. 'The police … I'm going to phone the police, so let go of me!'

But Mungo's grip on her arm grew tighter. He looked deeply into her eyes. 'The Lightning Tree. It is the way…'

Despite herself, Maggie sensed her resistance ebbing under Mungo's stare.

'It *is* the way,' he repeated, over and over again.

Try as she might, Maggie was unable to fight the weird, hypnotic effect of the old man's words, and she felt herself drifting into a trance. 'The Lightning Tree,' she whispered. 'It is the way. It *is* the way…'

* * *

MEANWHILE, IN ZORN'S UNDERGROUND LAIR...

Zorn was standing in front of his lofty throne, grinning smugly, while holding the terrified Charlie aloft by the scruff of the neck. He was surveying the scenes of misery below, where Keelie guards continued to lash lines of slaves with whips as they hauled wagons laden with coal through plumes of flame and choking smoke.

'Enough!' roared Zorn, though not as an act of mercy towards his victims. He made a flamboyant sweep of his arm. 'Rid the place of this stinking scum! *Away* with them! This is a time for celebration!' As his Keelie thugs drove the slaves, cringing and wailing, back into into their tunnel, Zorn guffawed in delight. 'Let there be music!' he bellowed. 'Merriment! Bring me wine!'

The deafening blare of heavy metal music filled the cavern. Green strobe lights flashed through billows of swirling vapour, and spurts of fire shot up in time with the beat. Zorn threw Charlie into the clutches of one of his midget sidekicks, before slumping back down on his throne. He took a deep slug from a goblet handed him by another flunky, then, with wine dribbling from the corners of his mouth, roared with manic laughter while the floor of his den swarmed with wildly-dancing headbangers from hell.

* * *

BACK IN TROWIE GLEN...

The grey clouds of morning were being brushed by flickers of lightning, while mutterings of thunder rumbled in the distance. Maggie, her hair and clothes buffeted by a brisk wind, was near the foot of the hill, looking towards its summit, where Mungo was standing under a dead tree – the Lightning Tree. Gazing skywards, hands outstretched, eyes closed, he was reciting an incantation, his words drowned out by the howling of the wind.

Maggie watched him raise his hands higher and higher, until a lightning bolt thudded with an ear-splitting crash into the upper branches of the tree. She staggered backwards, shielding her eyes with an arm.

'*The Power*!' Mungo shouted. '*Give me the Power*,

oh Mighty One!'

Rain lashed his face as ribbons of lightning spread down the tree and writhed over his body like electric snakes, rapidly enveloping him in a glittering, incandescent shroud. While smoke rose from the ground at the old man's feet, Maggie half turned away from the gale now blasting down from the hilltop.

But after a few moments the storm suddenly abated. Dark clouds gave way to a pale morning sky, and a strange stillness settled all around. Maggie ventured a glance over her shoulder and saw the aura that had been surrounding Mungo dissipate to reveal a male figure starting down the slope towards her. Although he was clad in a robe just like Mungo's, he did not have the old man's step or bearing. Indeed, as he drew closer, it became obvious to Maggie that the stranger was much, much younger, and notably better looking as well.

He stopped in front of Maggie. 'Well, Mistress McKim,' he smiled, 'we have an urgent task in hand, I believe?'

Maggie's reaction was a mix of puzzlement and alarm. 'But who *are* you? What happened to…? I – I mean, where is…?'

'Old Mungo?' the stranger chuckled. 'Why, I am he. Do you not recognise me?'

He motioned her to accompany him. But Maggie resisted. She was still feeling the dream-like effects of the spell old Mungo had cast on her, yet instinct was telling her to make a run for it, rather than risk going *any*where with this – this *apparition*.

Young Mungo could sense her misgivings, so knew he had to take control of the situation before the spell wore off completely. 'Do you not want to be reunited with your children?' he asked bluntly.

'Well, yes, but I – I –'

'Then, you must come with me immediately. There is no time to spare.'

Maggie's face was now a picture of total confusion. 'But I don't even know who you are. I mean, you say you're old Mungo, but how *can* you be?'

Mungo canted his head. 'Ah well, that is a long story – but one I confess you really *do* need to know.' He took her by the elbow. 'Come, Mistress McKim, I will tell you as we go.'

'Go? But – but go *where*, for heaven's sake?

'Why, to the castle of Goblin Hall, of course. Where else?'

* * *

BACK IN ZORN'S LAIR...

Zorn, still slouched on his throne, had his eyes fixed on the cloud 'screen' floating high above the swarms of Keelie goblins who were leaping and whirling to the beat of heavy metal music on the cavern floor. He was savouring live pictures of Susie and Jamie groping their way along the bat-infested tunnel that led from the stairway under the castle ruins. To his delight, Susie tripped over a rock and dropped her torch again. The clatter caused a swarm of bats to drop from their roost and flit blindly about.

'Excellent!' Zorn smirked while the children ducked and screamed. 'Now to make things *really* interesting for the obnoxious little runts!' He snapped his fingers, and the picture on the cloud began to shake violently.

In the tunnel, the children felt the ground tremble beneath their feet, as chunks of rock began to fall from the walls and roof. Then a large crack appeared in the floor behind Susie. Jamie shouted a warning, but too late to prevent his sister's feet from slipping over the edge of what was rapidly expanding into a yawning pit. At the bottom, a pair of giant, scaly, lizard-like creatures were lunging upwards, their mouths agape, saliva oozing from rows of razor-sharp teeth. Susie managed to grasp the edge of the pit with her fingertips, but knew she wouldn't be able to hold on for long. And those snapping jaws were getting closer to her ankles by the second.

'Oh *please*, Jamie,' she wailed. '*Do* something!'

Jamie threw himself down on his stomach, stretched over and grabbed one of her wrists. 'Don't ... don't move, Susie,' he panted. 'Just, uh ... just stay there.'

Normally, Susie wouldn't have been slow to let him know what she thought of his latest piece of silly advice, but she had more urgent matters to bother about right now. Her plight was made even worse by one of the creatures leaping up and snatching a leg of her jeans in its teeth. It only succeeded in tearing off a shred of cloth, but the tug was all it took to loosen her grip. Now Susie's very life depended on her little brother not letting her wrist slip through his fingers.

* * *

MEANWHILE, BACK INSIDE THE RUINED CASTLE...

Mungo came to the end of his tale while he and Maggie were picking their way over the rubble-strewn floor of the former great hall. 'So, you see, Mistress McKim, I can never invoke the Power from beneath the Lightning Tree in that way again. Only once in all the centuries of his life can a wizard do so. And in any case, without the other half of this sacred staff, which I carry in my robe always, the full *power* of the Power is denied me.'

But his explanations had only made Maggie more bewildered. 'The Power, wizards, goblins, Zorn. Honestly, this is all too … I don't know.' She shook her head. 'No, I – I think I'd better go to the police after all.'

Mungo gave her a cautionary look. 'Then you may never see your children again. Take my word for it – only I can rescue them from Zorn's dungeon of despair.'

Maggie was struggling to recover her trust in common sense. 'But why,' she countered, 'why should I believe all this?'

'Because what I tell you can only be possible *if* you believe!'

Maggie shook her head again. 'No, I'm sorry, I just can't accept –'

'You should have learned from your children,' Mungo butted in. 'Like all children, *they* believe. And so should you!'

Maggie was becoming more and more confused. 'But believe in *what*? Look, Susie and Jamie have disappeared, and – and you want me to trust someone who just stepped out of a thunderbolt!'

'The choice is yours, Mistress McKim.' Young Mungo couldn't have been more candid. 'Go and ask your police to help, if you must. However, I assure you that only I – with the strength of the Power behind me – have any chance of returning your children from Zorn's grasp. But if I fail, it will mean that he will finally have claimed the mantle of Great High Sorcerer for himself. The forces of evil will haunt the mortal world, and your children, if they survive, will be doomed to enslavement in the bowels of the earth for all time.'

'*If* they survive? What *exactly* do you mean by that?'

Mungo brushed her question aside. 'I have told you all I can, and time is running out.' He moved purposefully towards the concealed opening in the wall through which Susie and Jamie had been lured earlier. 'As I said before, this is now between Zorn and me, yet I assumed you would want to be with your children in their hour of need. Was I wrong?'

But Maggie was only half listening. Something on the floor had caught her eye. She stooped down and picked up a small plastic hair clip that was lying at the foot of the wall. 'This is Susie's, with – what's this? – with a little black feather caught in it.'

Mungo nodded his head knowingly. 'Stand aside, Mistress McKim. There is not a moment to spare.' He turned to face the rock 'door', one hand outstretched, fingers splayed, his head lowered, eyes unblinking. '*Apertabo porta – Zibanno*!' he shouted. A searing flash shot from his fingertips and crashed into the stone slab.

Maggie's heart skipped a beat. 'First thunderbolts, now firecrackers! What the blazes are you *playing* at?'

Mungo seemed not to hear. To his surprise, and no less dismay, the slab had not budged. He shouted the command again, but still the 'door' showed no sign of moving. Looking skywards, he mumbled an entreaty to the Mighty One, then braced himself, redoubled his concentration and pointed once more...

'*Oh ooblan, ooblan, baglan,*' he droned, his voice rising through '*apertabo porta*' to a crescendo of '*ZIBANNO!*'

An even more dazzling flash slammed into the slab of rock. Maggie cowered behind Mungo, who appeared oblivious to the hail of grit and gravel flying from the surface of the 'door' – which, in any event, remained stubbornly closed.

Zorn was watching all of this on his cloud 'screen', gloating over a close-up of little beads of sweat now glistening on Mungo's brow. 'Go on, you fool,' he muttered under his breath. 'Each feeble attempt you make is draining away more of your precious Power – *exactly* as I planned.' A smug grin spread over his face as Mungo attempted to blast the 'door' open yet again. This time, however, Zorn added an element of his own sorcery to the task. So, when the smoke from *this* lightning strike cleared, the stone slab shuddered and started to move – though only by an inch or two.

But it was enough to give Mungo heart. 'Yes! The Power is working!' he panted, then urgently repeated his incantation.

Although unknown to him, his words were echoed by Zorn, who grinned in malicious delight as he watched the 'door' grind slowly aside. 'Perfect!' he growled. 'Now to add more cheese to my trap.'

Meanwhile, Maggie peered into the eerie darkness of the stairway, then glared at Mungo. 'Are you suggesting that Susie and Jamie may have gone down … *there*?'

'I am *telling* you that they *did* go down there.' Mungo moved aside and beckoned her through. 'Well, shall we go? Or perhaps you would rather leave your little ones to Zorn's mercy – of which I can assure you he has none!'

Maggie's thoughts were in turmoil. She had never felt in such desperate need of Jim's presence as she did at this moment. He would have known what to do. But Jim was no longer by her side, and the cold reality of what that meant struck Maggie more chillingly now than at any time since his death. She felt utterly lost, drawn deeper and deeper into a nightmarish situation with no-one to turn to but this Mungo character. Again, her instincts were telling her to seek the help of the police, although there was still that strange feeling of not being fully in control of her own actions. But unreal as so many aspects of what was happening might seem, there was no denying that the little hair clip she now held in her hand was Susie's. Or was it? There were probably thousands of hair clips just like that one. And how could she be sure this weird stranger wasn't just making all these things happen by some sort of trickery? And for motives that might not be all that wholesome either! Come to think of it, why on earth should she be tempted to venture into a hidden passageway in a ruined castle with someone she had only just met, and under the most bizarre of circumstances as well? She should have gone straight to the police in the first place. Yes, and the more she thought about it, the more she was convinced it was still the most sensible thing to do.

But then she heard something that made her think again. It was a scream, the spine-chilling sound seeming to rise from somewhere deep beneath the very foundations of the castle. And immediately after, a child's voice calling for help echoed up from the same place.

'Susie?' Maggie gasped. 'Jamie? Oh, my God!'

The time for thinking was over. She made to head towards the stairs. But Mungo took hold of her arm.

'Let *go* of me!' she snapped. 'Those were my *children* you just heard!'

'I understand,' said Mungo, with a calmness in his voice that did nothing but infuriate Maggie all the more.

'But I've *got* to help them!'

'And so we will, Mistress McKim. But rushing headlong into this will do more harm than good.'

Maggie tried to push past him.

'Just calm down,' Mungo said softly, 'and do as I say.'

'Calm *down*? You expect me to be calm when – when –'

Mungo laid a placating hand on hers. 'Hopefully, no real harm will befall you or your children.'

'*Hopefully*?' Maggie tried to free herself. 'No! Get out of my *way*! Let me *past*!'

Young Mungo gripped Maggie's shoulders and held her at arms' length, fixing her in an unblinking stare. Maggie realised in an instant that his eyes mirrored the look that 'old' Mungo had mesmerised her with earlier. But there was something else about his eyes that seemed familiar. Something she felt she should have been able to place, yet somehow couldn't. Not that it mattered anyway. All that concerned Maggie right now was that her children were in danger and she had to find them – quickly, even if it meant going along with the advice of this mystery man who claimed to be some sort of reincarnation of that other robe-wearing oddball.

Mungo could understand her confused state of mind. 'Trust me ... please,' he said. 'You are about to enter a world of black magic, of sorcery of the darkest kind. So, you must believe in the good and deny the bad.' He paused for a moment, then added solemnly: 'And remember, not *every*thing will be as it seems. Do you understand?'

Maggie didn't know what the blazes he was talking about. But she had no choice. She duly nodded her head, and the moment he released her, she motioned him to lead the way, crossed her fingers, then stepped into the unknown.

* * * * *

– CHAPTER NINE –

DEEP BENEATH THE CASTLE RUINS...

Although Susie and Jamie's cries had horrified Maggie, they were music to Zorn's ears, a source of malicious pleasure to savour while he watched the ordeals he was creating come to life on his cloud 'screen'.

Susie's worst fears had been realised, but not because Jamie had let her wrist slip through his fingers. Indeed, he was still holding onto it as they lay sprawled together on the floor of the pit. They'd tumbled in because Zorn had made the ground give way under Jamie as he struggled to pull his sister out of the giant lizards' reach. And to make matters worse, Zorn had also plunged the pit into darkness.

The children scrambled to their knees, hugging each other, trying desperately to catch a glimpse of the fearsome creatures they knew were lurking somewhere in the black silence that surrounded them. After a few agonising moments, there emerged from the gloom a sinister hissing noise – distant at first, but getting closer by the second. Suddenly, a hideous reptilian face burst from the darkness. With the ground quaking beneath its feet, the monster closed in, breathing fire, yellow eyes blazing, mighty jaws gaping to expose rows of teeth capable of crushing two children in one bite.

Susie and Jamie could only hold each other tightly, too petrified to even call for help. They shut their eyes, their hearts racing as they awaited the awful fate about to descend on them.

Lounging on his throne, Zorn was in raptures of delight, pointing at his 'screen' and spluttering with laughter as he gulped down another slug of wine. 'Look at the cringing brats!' he wheezed to his Keelie attendants. 'Fantastic! This is priceless entertainment! Yes, and the fun and games are only just beginning!' He popped his fingers and shouted, '*Mutabbo conneckos!*'

On the 'screen', the scene changed from the squalor of the pit to a rolling meadow, on which the sun was shining from a clear blue sky, and rabbits nibbled grass while hopping around the patch where Susie and Jamie lay. To complete this pastoral idyll, birdsong had replaced the hissing and spitting of giant lizards, with the sweet aroma of wild flowers dispelling the awful stench of reptile droppings.

Hesitantly, the children opened their eyes, blinking into the sunlight, unable to comprehend the miraculous change in their surroundings. They helped each other up and stared all around, marvelling at the beauty of the place, though fearful that the blood-curdling sounds of hidden monsters might yet shatter the atmosphere of peace and well-being. But all they could hear was the far-off barking of a dog. A small one.

Jamie shaded his eyes and peered into the distance. 'Can you see anything, Susie? I *think* it sounds like Charlie, but...'

Susie followed his gaze for a few seconds. 'It *is* Charlie!' she said. 'Look there, Jamie! On that little hill – over there on the far side of the meadow! It's Charlie! It *is*!'

Jamie could hardly contain himself. 'CHARLIE!' he yelled, waving both hands above his head. 'Come here, Charlie! It's *us*! Come on now – there's a good boy!'

Still barking, Charlie wagged his tail, but instead of running towards his two young chums, he turned, trotted off happily in the opposite direction and disappeared over the top of the hill.

The children were completely dumbfounded.

'Where's he *go*ing?' Susie gasped.

Jamie came to a swift conclusion. 'I think he maybe knows where Jasper's at. Wants us to follow him.'

Susie wasn't so sure. Even though she had no way of knowing that all these bewildering events were being created by Zorn, her big-sisterly intuition told her there was something fishy going on. 'Hmm,' she frowned, tapping a sceptical forefinger on her top lip. 'Hmm.'

'No time to "hmm"!' Jamie declared. 'Charlie wants us to go with him, so let's *go*!'

Without further ado, Jamie was off at the gallop.

Susie shouted after her little brother, pleading with him to stop. But her pleas fell on deaf ears. What now? Susie was in a flap. She took a quick look around. As pleasant as it all appeared, she couldn't get rid of the creepy feeling that everything could change back in an instant to what it had been a few minutes ago. And the last place she wanted to be was in that den of monsters – alone.

'Wait for me, Jamie!' she hollered. 'I'm coming too!'

* * *

BACK IN THE UNDERGROUND PASSAGE...

Maggie and Mungo were approaching the area where Zorn had terrified the children with a minor earthquake, before dumping them into what at first had *seemed* to be a pit inhabited by giant, man-eating reptiles.

Mungo led Maggie by the hand through piles of rubble, then stopped, his ear cocked to a faint but steady thumping sound, which was accompanied by a sort of raspy screeching. 'What fiendish cacophony is *that*?'

Maggie listened for a moment. 'Just heavy metal,' she shrugged.

Mungo squinted at her. 'Heavy ... *metal*?'

'Yes – you know – hard rock music. Must be a nightclub down here somewhere.'

Mungo's brows gathered into a frown. '*Music*? The tuneless caterwauling of demons, more like!'

'So, you're not a Led Zeppelin fan then? Iron Maiden maybe?' Maggie studied his look of utter puzzlement, then ran an eye over his long, flowing robe. She shook her head. 'No, I don't suppose you'd have done any headbanging yourself, come to think of it.'

Mungo stroked his chin. 'Metal music as hard as rock, airships that would be too heavy to fly, young ladies made of iron who bang heads together...?' His frown deepened. 'I have not heard such strange utterances since I levitated a piglet when I was but an apprentice to the previous Great High Sorcerer. Yes, and the piglet had an excuse – he spoke in a strange tongue called American, but many centuries before anyone talked that way. Mmm, bummer, funky, groovy, party pooper – words like that.'

Well, thought Maggie, she really *had* heard it all now. First it had been a flying mouse, now a levitated piglet – whatever that was – which could not only talk, but talk American slang before any such lingo existed. Anyhow, even if Maggie had had the time to ask Mungo for an explanation, what happened next would have made her choke on her words.

She let out an ear-splitting shriek as a huge spider dropped from the ceiling and scurried across her face.

'Sh-h-h!' Mungo hissed, still standing with his ear cocked. 'There's something else...'

Maggie shrieked again as a snake slid out of the shadows and slithered over her foot.

Mungo glared at her. 'Sh-h-h! Listen!'

'But spiders – snakes! I can't *stand* them!'

'Quiet ... please!'

Maggie took a deep breath, made a valiant effort to pull herself together, then stood shaking in her shoes – but silently.

And true enough, there was something else: another sound, mixed in with the muffled thump of rock music. A nearer sound, and less raucous too. A grunting, gnashing, slobbering sound, coming from somewhere a bit further along the tunnel.

Maggie shuddered. 'What in heaven's name *is* it?'

Mungo held a finger to his lips, then proceeded to lead the way onward, one wary step at a time. The mysterious noises grew louder as they neared the pit into which the children had fallen.

'Careful,' said Mungo. 'The ground here is crumbling away.'

Maggie didn't have to be told twice. Holding onto Mungo's arm for support, she leaned forward just far enough to see over the rim of the pit, then screwed her face up. 'Oh, my God, how revolting! Look – just *look* at those creatures down there – those horrible, slimy, lizard-looking monsters...'

'Not lizards, but dragons, Mistress McKim. Or what mortals might call dinosaurs.' Mungo took a closer look. 'Hmm, a type of Allosaurus, perhaps. Or even some sort of cross between a Stegosaurus and a Velociraptor. No matter, I always maintain a dragon by any other name is still a dragon, even flightless ones like those appear to –'

'OK, whatever!' Maggie was in no mood to listen to a long-winded lecture on prehistoric wildlife. 'Look, all I know is they're devouring great lumps of raw meat, all bloody and – and they're tearing the skin off it with their claws!' She turned her head away, trying not to throw up.

Mungo patted her arm. 'Do not distress yourself, Mistress McKim. Remember what I told you – not *every*thing may be as it appears.'

It was obvious from Maggie's expression that she still hadn't the faintest idea what he was talking about.

Mungo smiled patiently. 'Those creatures, those dragons – they may not be real, you see – merely a trick of Zorn's – an optical illusion.'

'An *illusion*?' Maggie gave a little snort. 'You can't be serious, surely!'

'Oh, but I am.' Mungo could not have been more emphatic. 'Please permit me to demonstrate.' He bent down and picked up a lump of rock. 'Observe, and you will see what I mean.' He took careful aim and threw the rock into the pit, hitting one of the creatures squarely on top of its skull. *Kudonk*!

Though perhaps more irritated than hurt, the beast snarled, looked up through eyes that oozed vengeance, then duly hurled the rock right back.

Mungo ducked as the missile whizzed past his ear and smashed in a thousand pieces on the wall behind him. He shook the grit from his hair and faked a cough. 'It, ehm – it would appear,' he said through a sheepish smile, 'that the creatures are real after all.'

Maggie raised an eyebrow, but held her tongue, concentrating instead on stemming her feeling of nausea before venturing another peek into the pit. 'The skin they're tearing off that flesh,' she said, gagging. 'Look, it's pink. *Pink*!'

'Hmm,' Mungo nodded. 'A pig, most likely.'

While Maggie watched aghast, one of the creatures ripped what looked like a small leg bone from the flesh and began using it as a toothpick to remove a shred of cloth that had become snagged in its fangs. With a jerk of its head, the beast flicked the blood-soaked remnant upwards to land at Maggie's feet. She noticed immediately that it wasn't just any old rag. It was a piece of blue denim.

Maggie glowered at Mungo, tears welling in her eyes. 'A pig, you say. A pig – wearing *jeans*?' She buried her face in her hands as the full significance of what she had just witnessed struck home. 'Please, God, no,' she sobbed. 'It can't be. It *can't* be...'

Mungo placed an arm round her shoulders. 'Do not torture yourself,' he murmured soothingly. 'Such a deed would not be Zorn's way, believe me.' He paused to look sidelong into the pit, his expression grim. 'No, he is more devious than that. Much more devious than that.'

'How right you are,' Zorn muttered in the secrecy of his cavern. 'How right you are, you pathetic milksop.' He allowed himself a self-satisfied smirk, before snapping his fingers to change the scene on the cloud 'screen' yet again...

* * *

BACK IN THE GRASSY MEADOW...

The sun was still shining, the birds singing cheerily

as Jamie reached the top of the hill over which Charlie the dog had disappeared. He stopped abruptly, scarcely able to believe his eyes. Susie arrived breathless at his side, her reaction to what she saw mirroring his own. They were overlooking a ravine, with a raging torrent at the bottom, and cliffs rising sheer and high on either side. To the children's dismay, Charlie was standing shivering on a rocky outcrop in the middle of the rapids, his tail between his legs, his eyes imploring them to come to his rescue. But there was no way.

'Oh, Charlie,' Susie whimpered, 'how on *earth* did you get yourself into such a pickle?'

'Bet I know,' Jamie scowled. 'Bet that bad man who stole Jasper magicked him there.'

'How right you are,' Zorn smirked in his lair. 'How right you are, you insignificant little worm!'

Susie turned to look back over the meadow, hoping to see something, *any*thing they could use to help save Charlie. But the sight that greeted her made her heart sink. She nudged her little brother. '*Please* tell me I'm seeing things, Jamie.'

But Jamie was just as bewildered as she was. Instead of the lush landscape they had just left, there was a desert, an arid ocean of sand dunes rolling away as far as the eye could see. The children looked at each other, then down towards Charlie. They stood in silence, wrapped in a shroud of despair. After a while, Jamie touched his sister's elbow.

'Susie?' he said in a timid voice.

'Uh-huh?' Susie replied, while continuing to stare forlornly at the tiny island where Charlie was marooned.

'Susie?' Jamie said again.

'Uh-huh?'

'I – uhm – I think I need a poop!'

* * *

MEANWHILE, BACK IN THE UNDERGROUND PASSAGE...

Maggie's disgust at what she had seen in the pit was soon overcome by her maternal instinct to find her children and protect them from whatever dangers they were being exposed to. And even though she couldn't fathom why this Mungo fellow kept going on about the mysterious Zorn, about good-versus-bad and not *every*thing they saw being real, he was her only source of support, so there was nothing else for it but to place her trust in him. It wasn't long, however, before her confidence in his ability to measure up was severely tested...

They had only just eased their way past the mouth of the dragons' pit when a solid wall of stone suddenly rose up in front of them.

'Oh, no,' Maggie groaned. 'I can't believe this is happening.'

'Then believe *this*, my beauty!' Zorn countered. He nodded at Maggie's image on the cloud 'screen', and behind her the roof of the tunnel began to collapse in a deluge of rocks. The passageway had now become totally blocked, in both directions.

While Maggie stood transfixed, Mungo put on a brave front, albeit none too credibly. 'Do not – I mean, *try* not to fret, Mistress McKim. Zorn, you know – perhaps just another of his dirty tricks – an illusion.'

'Well, it's a pretty convincing one, if you ask me!' Maggie's eyes darted from side to side. 'Admit it – we're entombed!'

Mungo stepped forward and ran his hands over the face of the wall. He then stepped back and surveyed it for a few seconds, before stepping forward again to tap it in several places with his knuckles. He shrugged his shoulders and heaved a resigned sort of sigh. *'Ho-hum*, not a fake after all, it would appear.'

His apparent acceptance of their fate inflamed Maggie so much that she turned and lifted a lump of rock from the caved-in roof, then threw it clattering to the floor. 'And neither is this. Polystyrene doesn't make a noise like that, in case you were wondering.'

'Poly … who?'

'Styrene! Poly*styrene*!'

Mungo stared at her, blankly.

'Oh, forget it!' Maggie closed her eyes and clapped a hand to her forehead. *'Please*, someone wake me up in my own bed and promise me this has all been a bad dream!'

She felt a hand patting her shoulder, but on opening her eyes was disappointed – yet not too surprised – to find she was still in the tunnel, with Mungo standing in front of her. Although they were now in almost total darkness, she could tell he had a reassuring smile on his face.

'There, there,' he crooned. 'Believe in the good and deny the bad.'

Maggie shook her head in frustration. 'Fat chance! How the blazes do you expect me to believe in the good when there's nothing but bad happening?'

Mungo was all set to resume sermonising when a grating sound drew their attention to the stone wall. It had started to move towards them. Maggie tried to persuade herself that she was seeing things, but had to admit that, slowly but surely, the space between the wall in front of them and the rockfall behind them was shrinking.

'What do you suggest I believe in now?' she enquired as calmly as she could. 'I'm denying it as hard as I can, but that damned wall is still moving!'

Mungo pursed his lips. 'Hmm, I take your point, Mistress McKim. It, uhm – it does indeed appear that we may have a slight problem in that regard.'

'Well, *do* something!'

Mungo scratched the back of his head. 'Yes, I – I'm considering the options, mistress.'

'*Options*?' Maggie was becoming frantic. 'Listen, there are no op*tions* to consider. You either get us out of this, or we'll be squashed like flies. Op*tion*, singular!'

'Yes, it – it would indeed appear so.'

'Well?'

Mungo was stroking his chin now.

'Oh, for heaven's sake!' Maggie snapped. 'Look, walls of solid stone don't just move of their own accord.

It's obviously some sort of conjuring jiggery-pokery, trumped up by this Zorn bloke, whoever he is.'

Mungo, apparently still contemplating his options, didn't reply. But the wall kept moving relentlessly towards them.

'Come on then,' Maggie goaded. 'You claim to be a magician, so –'

'Wizard!' Mungo interjected, and indignantly so. 'I'm a wizard, *not* a magician. There *is* a difference, Mistress McKim.'

'Fine, but spare me the details for now if you don't mind, and just *do* something, for Pete's sake!'

'Pete?' Mungo was scratching his head again. 'Who is Pete?'

All this shilly-shallying was beginning to drive Maggie potty. Grimacing, she reached out and touched the wall, which was already getting uncomfortably close. 'Just – just – oh, I don't know – just do the same routine – you know, spout the same mumbo-jumbo you did to get us into this awful place. Just chuck one of your fireworks at the wall and shout "*Xanadu*" or whatever!'

'Ah, you mean invoke the Power?' Mungo gave an indulgent little laugh. 'I'm afraid it isn't as simple as that. You see, if I draw on more of my reserves now, I may not have enough left to match Zorn when –'

'OK, OK! You've gone over all that stuff before. But what good will your precious Power be when we're the filling in a rock sandwich? Which, by the look of things, will be in about a couple of minutes from now!'

Mungo was on the horns of a dilemma, but was

obliged to concede that standing around considering non-existent options would get them nowhere. 'Yes, point taken, Mistress McKim. We do indeed find ourselves between a rock and a hard place, as the, uhm, as the saying goes. Now, uh, if you would...' He stepped aside to allow Maggie to move behind him. Bracing himself, he adopted the required stance, then raised a hand, fingers splayed, pointing at the wall. Anxious moments passed as he continued to ready himself, taking deep breaths, moaning, summoning up his strength. In the meantime, the wall was crunching ever closer.

'Get a *move* on!' Maggie shouted. Struggling not to panic, she staggered back against the rockfall, staring wide-eyed at the approaching barrier of stone.

'*Oh-h-h, ooblan balnagab,*' Mungo eventually began. '*Oh-h-h,* o*oblan muraba sistabo,*' he continued, his voice rising to a higher pitch with every word. Then, with a shout of '*Zibanno!*', he released from his fingertips a bolt of lightning that sent sparks and chunks of stone flying from the surface of the wall.

Yet still it kept inching forward.

Maggie closed her eyes, afraid to look.

'*Zibanno!*' Mungo repeated, though more urgently this time. '*Muraba sistabo!*

Another flash blasted into the wall, but once again failed to stop it. Mungo was now looking distinctly worried. Although he knew it would be costing him valuable reserves of the Power, he tried over and over again to halt the advancing sheet of stone, which was now almost touching his outstretched hand. But his efforts came to nothing. Sweating profusely, he took a faltering step backwards and slumped, gasping for breath, against the rockfall next to Maggie.

'It – it's no good,' he panted. 'I can't seem to...'

'Keep trying!' Maggie urged. 'You've *got* to!' She could see that he was in a state of near collapse, but his 'mumbo-jumbo', as she'd so disparagingly called it, was their only hope. 'Go on!' she shouted. 'Say it again! Say "*Maroobo*" or whatever!'

Mungo strained every muscle to raise his hand, then pointed his shaking fingers once more at the wall. '*Mur-mura-muraba*,' he began, but was unable to complete the incantation before his hand flopped limply to his side. 'I – I'm sorry, mistress,' he stammered, 'I seem to have lost the ability to...'

Maggie was at her wits' end. She grabbed his hand and lifted it up. 'Say it all! Say the rest of the words!'

But it was too late. With a grinding jolt, the wall lurched suddenly forward, pushing their hands back and forcing their shoulders hard against the rockfall. A horrific death was now only inches away. And the wall continued its relentless advance.

In desperation, Mungo could only lean against it and push with what little strength he had left.

Zorn, watching live images in his lair deep below, uttered a menacing chuckle. 'You fool, Mungo,' he sneered. 'You are draining away your supply of the Power, exactly as I planned. Ah, but I have not finished with you yet.' He snapped his fingers and the wall disappeared in a swirl of dust, leaving Mungo lying face down on the floor of the tunnel.

Zorn was laughing so much he almost choked on his wine. 'On your feet, pipsqueak!' he barked. 'I'm not letting you off *that* lightly! No indeed, but first I must see to those snivelling mortal brats…'

* * * * *

– CHAPTER TEN –

BACK AT THE EDGE OF THE RAVINE...

The children were still gazing dejectedly down to the tiny island where Charlie was stranded.

'Susie, *you*'ll have to go and fetch him,' Jamie said at length.

'Why me?'

''Cause I can't swim.'

Susie puffed out her cheeks and pointed a finger at the rushing water that held their little dog prisoner. 'Well, *I*'m not trying to swim in *that*!'

Jamie thought for a bit, then said, 'What are we going to do, then?'

Stumped for ideas, Susie could only shrug.

Equally at a loss, Jamie frowned, stuffed his hands in his pockets and continued to think. Then his face lit up.

'Why are you looking so happy all of a sudden?' asked Susie, frowning herself now. 'And don't tell me it's got something to do with the poop you said you were needing to do.'

Treating that catty remark with the disdain he felt it deserved, Jamie took from his pocket the two gold

coins Jake the jackdaw had dropped into his hand at
the entrance to the underground passage.

Susie's face lit up now too. 'The magic money!'

The children stared at the coins, then looked each
other in the eye, ideas hatching.

Jamie was first to speak. 'Maybe, if we say old
Mungo's magic word...'

Susie frowned again. 'Maybe what?'

Jamie hunched his shoulders. '*I* don't know.' He
thought some more. 'Well, maybe –'

'Maybe, maybe, maybe,' Susie butted in, 'maybe
we'll finish up back in that horrible pit, that's what!'

Jamie shook his head. 'Don't think so.'

'How do *you* know?'

''Cause the pit was bad.'

'And?'

'And these are good pennies.'

Susie was clearly not persuaded. She tapped her
top lip again, weighing things up.

Jamie prodded her arm. 'Go on, Susie – say the
magic word!'

Though with some reluctance, Susie was beginning
to come round to his way of thinking. In any case,
what choice did they have? 'Well, I *suppose* it's
worth a try,' she conceded, then adopted her bossy,
big-sisterly attitude again. 'But *you*'ll have to say it!'

'Can't.'

'Why not?'

'Forgotted it.'

'Typical!' Susie tutted. 'Honestly, you're *so* unreliable
at times.'

Jamie's patience was rapidly running out. 'OK

then, *you* tell me the word and *I*'ll say it!'

'Can't!'

'Why not?'

Susie gave her little brother a haughty look. 'Just because.'

Jamie glowered at her through narrowed eyes. 'You've forgotted the word too, haven't you?'

'Well, yes, if you *must* know.' Susie raised her nose in the air. 'But only because *I* wasn't really listening to old Mungo's hocus-pocus back at his cottage, that's why.'

'Typical!' Jamie tutted. 'You're *so* un-re-liar-bubble at times. *And* you tell fibs.'

A tense silence ensued while the children resumed their vigil over the rock on which their little dog was marooned.

'Still can't understand how Charlie got there,' Susie said after a while.

'Swimmed?' Jamie suggested.

Susie shot him a don't-be-silly look.

'Maybe flied then.'

'Dogs can't fly,' Susie scoffed.

Jamie pondered the conundrum some more, then nodded his head. 'That's why I think somebody magicked him there. And I still think it was the bad man that stole Jasper.' He glanced at his sister, fully expecting his latest suggestion to be rubbished too.

But Susie was deep in thought, tapping her top lip again. 'Maybe,' she said under her breath, 'just maybe...' She gave Jamie a nudge. '*That* could be the answer!'

Jamie was all ears, though becoming more

confused by the minute.

Susie was buzzing with excitement. 'You know, the same as Aladdin did with his lamp, remember?'

'No.'

'Well, if you rub a coin and – and –'

'Uh-huh?'

'Well, if you rub a coin and make a wish that Charlie could fly, maybe he'll be magicked back up here. See what I mean?'

Jamie didn't really see what she meant, but wasted no time in starting to rub one of the coins anyway – while also keeping his eyes tightly closed to facilitate maximum concentration.

'Are you remembering to wish?' Susie checked.

'Yes, wishing really hard.'

'Well, wish even *harder*!'

'Is he flying yet?'

'No! Rub harder! Keep wishing!'

'You wish too then.'

Susie decided that her brother had finally spoken sense, so promptly set about giving him some back-up.

Jamie half opened his eyes and peeked across at Charlie. 'He's still not flying, Susie.'

'Close your eyes again and rub harder then!'

'Finger's getting sore.'

'Doesn't matter – keep going!'

Jamie gave a little moan. 'Think my finger's catching fire though.'

Without any warning, Susie gripped his arm, tightly. 'I've *got* it!' she shouted.

'What? A fire stingwisher?'

'No, the magic word! It's – it's ...' Susie took a deep breath, then her voice cut through the torrent's roar like the shriek of a banshee. '*Zibanno-o-o-o!*' she yelled. Then once more for good measure: '*ZIBANNO-O-O-O!*'

In an instant, there was a dazzling flash of light high above the ravine, followed by a loud '*BANG!*'. The children gaped open-mouthed as, out of the smoky aftermath of the explosion, there appeared a strange winged creature, gliding down unsteadily in their direction. As it got closer, they were astonished to see that the creature was actually a small pig, which reminded them immediately of the slang-speaking American piglet old Mungo had described when telling of his experiences as a trainee wizard.

'*Wilbur?*' they gasped in unison.

In his cavern, a smug Zorn was encouraging a bunch of Keelie goblins to look at this bizarre encounter on his cloud 'screen'. 'Who but I could have thought of *that?*' he smirked. 'The meeting of a show-off flying ham and two gullible little swine.' His toady minions twisted their faces into grins of approval. 'But if you think that is brilliant,' Zorn went on, 'prepare to feast your eyes on what I have in store for them next...'

As Wilbur continued to glide earthward, his zig-zagging flight path and the pained expression on his face suggested that he was far from being in control. Prudently, Susie and Jamie took a couple of steps back.

'Hey, kids!' the piglet shouted. 'What's happenin'?

Where *am* I already?'

Before they could tell him they hadn't a clue themselves, Wilbur let out a yodel-like squeal and crash-landed nearby in a somersaulting blur of legs and wings. Not wishing to lose face, he struggled quickly to his feet.

'Jeez, freaky trip!' he beamed, 'I mean, one minute I'm on the movie set doin' a love scene with this porky puppet chick...' He savoured the thought for a moment.

'I bet he means Miss Piggy!' Susie whispered excitedly in Jamie's ear. 'You know – her in the Muppets!'

'...and then,' Wilbur continued, '*Blam*! Next thing, the wings sprout and I'm flyin' around out here in the sticks. What gives, huh?'

Susie tried not to look too awestruck in the presence of such a well-connected celebrity. 'We don't know anything,' she confessed with a coy smile. 'We, ehm, we're only here to save Charlie.'

Wilbur tilted his head to one side. 'Charlie? Who the sage 'n' onion stuffin' is Charlie?'

Susie nodded in the direction of their destitute pet.

'Can you help us?' Jamie pleaded. '*Please*?'

Wilbur took one look at the tumbling rapids and immediately sussed the situation. 'Aw, hey, no way, boy! Nah, nah – include me outta this! Pigs and water? *Woah* – bad mix!'

Jamie's disappointment was suppressed, temporarily at least, by his fascination with this most unusual of animals. He scrutinised Wilbur from snout to tail, then asked bluntly, 'You *really* in the movies?'

Wilbur did the piglet equivalent of sticking his chest out. 'Yeah, yeah – oh, for sure, yeah.' He rolled his shoulders in a swaggering sort of way. 'I mean, ya musta seen me in that old James Bond flick – 007 – Roger Moore. *You* know, the one with the fat sheriff chewin' the chewin' tabacca and spittin'?' He paid no heed to the children's blank expressions. 'Yeah, sure ya did! Well, *I* was that fat sheriff. Recognise me now?' When this still failed to produce a positive reaction, he cleared his throat and blustered, 'Right, OK, it *was* heavy make-up, I'll give ya that. But, yeah, a great part for me, *and* they wrote me some swell lines as well. Like when I says to Bond, "Hey, you're that secret agent, ain'cha?"' He treated himself to a smug smile. 'Yessiree, they don't write lines like that too often … well, not for pigs anyways.'

All this bragging was beginning to arouse Susie's suspicions. Time, she decided, to lob the piglet a loaded question. 'Do your own stunts as well, do you?'

Wilbur took the bait, hook, line and sinker. 'Aw, yeah – no problem, honey. Nah, they never need no stand-ins for Wilbur when they're shootin' life-threatenin' scenes. No way! Yeah, I mean, even in that Bond movie I was talkin' about, it was me had to double for the Moore guy when –'

'Why are you scared to rescue Charlie then?'

Susie's timely intrusion took the wind right out of Wilbur's sails, but he quickly covered up by feigning disbelief. 'Scared? *Me* scared? Get outta here!'

Jamie glowered at him. 'Fly down and get Charlie then.'

Wilbur immediately went on the defensive. 'Fly down and get Charlie, he says! Yeah, yeah, just fly down and pick him up, Wilbur, right? *Hmmff*! Well, let me tell ya – pigs trotters is good for may things, kiddo, but pickin' up puppy dogs ain't one a' them. Darned right it ain't! *And* before ya say anything else, I gotta point out that this cute little body a' mine ain't fitted out with no air-sea rescue equipment neither.' He watched the children's expressions change from disappointment to total disillusionment, and realised he was in real danger of blowing the fearless-hero image he'd been trying so hard to cultivate. 'I mean, let's face it, guys,' he said, sounding slightly more apologetic than assertive, 'a helicopter I ain't.'

Jamie turned his back on him and asked Susie what Aladdin would have done in a situation like this. His sister replied that, when rubbed, Aladdin's lamp had produced a very helpful genie, while Jake the jackdaw's coins had only come up with a very *un*helpful pig.

'Yes,' she added with a disdainful glance in Wilbur's direction, 'and a cowardly one at that!'

Her comment was intended to hit Wilbur where it hurt most – smack dab on his vanity button. And the ploy worked.

'Hey, hey, cool it!' he snapped. 'What gives with the cowardly bit, huh?'

Susie had him on the ropes now, and she wasn't going to waste a second in delivering the knock-out punch, even if it meant telling a fib or two to add the required amount of sting. 'Old Mungo the wizard told us all about you,' she said blandly.

Wilbur's jaw dropped. 'Ya sayin' ya know *Mungo*?'

Susie indicated the affirmative.

Wilbur gulped. 'Ya referrin' to the same Mungo they made the actual Great High Sorcerer way back?'

'Yes, and he told us about when you were in the wizards' school in Goblin Hall Castle long, long ago, and how all the students loved you because you did so many brave things.'

'He said *that*?' Wilbur was clearly struggling to believe his ears.

'Certainly did,' said Susie. 'Didn't he, Jamie?'

It was at moments like this that Jamie was glad he had an older, wiser sister to guide him through the subtleties of life. 'Cert'ly did,' he concurred.

Looking distinctly stunned, Wilbur pulled a lop-sided smile. 'Wow! How *about* that?'

Susie allowed him a few moments to wallow in this puddle of praise, then hit him with a body blow. 'But Mungo is going to be very sad when we tell him you're not so brave any more.'

Wilbur's jaw dropped again – but farther this time. 'Ya tellin' me ye're gonna see Mungo *again* sometime?'

'Certainly are. Going to meet him later today, in fact. Aren't we Jamie?'

'Cert'ly are.'

Susie smelled blood, so went in for the kill. 'Yes, and we'll tell him to spread the word *every*where that you refused to help us save the life of our poor wee dog Charlie.'

Wilbur shuffled his trotters and huffed and puffed a bit. 'W-well now,' he flustered, 'just, uhm, just hold on a truffle-rootlin' minute there, kids. I – I guess maybe we should take another look at this here situation.' He offered the children a cheesy smile. 'Now then, what *exactly* was the problem again?'

Susie wagged an admonishing finger at him. 'You know very well what the problem is, so stop mucking about. Are you, or are you not, going to fly down for Charlie?'

'I'll come with you, if you want,' Jamie chipped in. 'Keep you company.'

Wilbur wrinkled his snout. 'Ah well, ya see, I ain't accustomed to havin' kids ridin' piggy-back – if you'll pardon the expression.'

'Never too late to learn,' said Susie, and promptly lent her brother a steadying hand while he swung a leg over the piglet's shoulders.

A minute later, a browbeaten Wilbur was airborne again, nose-diving out of control towards the torrent, with Jamie, arms flailing, straddled precariously on his back.

'The wings!' Wilbur yelled. 'Don't foul the wings, kid! It's crampin' ma flappin'!'

Jamie closed his eyes as they zoomed vertically downwards.

Susie, fearing she was about to be left brotherless, pressed her hands to her ears and started to scream. Though faint, Susie's cries could be heard back in the tunnel, where Maggie and young Mungo were recovering from the terrifying ordeal they'd been subjected to by Zorn.

'What was that?' said Maggie, peering into the darkness of the passageway ahead.

'I didn't hear anything,' Mungo replied, breathless and bruised from his struggle with the wall, but hurting most from the indignity of having fallen flat on his face at the end of it.

Maggie was straining her ears. 'There it is again! That sound – it's a scream – a child's scream!'

'Most likely only bats,' said Mungo, his intention being to spare Maggie the anguish that can result from jumping too quickly to conclusions. But it had the opposite effect.

'For your information,' she retorted, 'I *can* tell the difference between a child and a bat. Oh, and another thing, if you tell me one more time that not *every*thing may be as it as it seems, I'll start screaming myself!'

'*BWA-A-A-AH*!' Jamie bellowed, holding on to Wilbur's ears for dear life as the piglet finally managed to pull out of his dive, mere inches above the thundering waters of the torrent. He beat his wings furiously in an effort to gain height while they careered around erratically within the craggy confines of the ravine.

Up on the edge, Susie had only just found the courage to squint through her fingers when Wilbur attempted his first approach to the tiny rock on which Charlie was trapped. She screamed again as the piglet overshot his target and skimmed so low over the rapids that Jamie's feet trailed in the water.

But undaunted – or at least making a commendable show of faking it – Wilbur redoubled his efforts and succeeded in climbing to an altitude that seemed sufficient to allow another downwards swoop towards Charlie.

'Listen up, kid,' he called over his shoulder. 'Regard that as a dry run – if, uh, you'll pardon the expression. Anyhow, I ain't equipped with no vertical landin' and take-off gear, so this time, when I pull outta the dive, you lean over and snatch the pooch. Roger?'

Jamie was so shaken up he could hardly breathe. 'My n-name's n-not Roger!' he spluttered.

'So *what*? We're talkin' aviatin' talk here! So, are ya cool for grabbin' the mutt on a full-speed fly-past or ain'cha?'

'Y-yes … th-think so.'

'Don't think, buddy. Just *do* it! Now, here we go…!'

Within the first few seconds of their descent, however, Wilbur had lost control again, albeit that he refused to admit it. 'OK, junior,' he shouted to Jamie as they plummeted earthward like a shot-down fighter plane, 'we're lookin' good! Get yer mitt ready to scoop up the mutt!'

Jamie closed his eyes again. The only other time he had felt his heart skipping beats like this was when they'd gone on a family holiday to the seaside and went for a roller coaster ride at the funfair. He'd been scared on that occasion as well, but not as scared as this. Back then, someone had wrapped a protecting arm around his shoulders: someone who would keep him safe from harm – always and everywhere. He felt tears welling in his eyes as he thought of his Daddy and wished he were here now.

This was precisely the thought going through Susie's mind as she turned her head away, unable to watch the inevitable crash from which her little brother would be unlikely to emerge alive.

Yet, nail-biting moments later, it wasn't howls of distress that echoed up from the bottom of the gorge, but a wobbly sounding '*Woa-a-a-ah*!' as Wilbur soared skyward, riding an updraft of warm air like a portly, pink eagle.

'Bum deal!' he grunted. 'Didn't reckon on hittin' no thermals!' But the hint of a smile tugging at the corner of his mouth suggested he was actually more relieved than annoyed.

Jamie, who was still holding on like grim death to the piglet's ears, didn't know what had happened while he wasn't looking, but was extremely grateful that it had. Even so, hitting the thermals, whatever they were, hadn't helped save poor Charlie, and he was quick to remind Wilbur of the fact.

'Yeah, no sweat,' the piglet panted as the force of gravity began to drag them down again. 'But – *phew*! – really gotta be this time, boy. I'm one pooped pig!'

Whether more by fluke than design, the piglet now employed a new tactic, sweeping wide of the rock to make his approach from downstream at a gentle angle of descent. Watching from the bank, Susie could see Wilbur gliding over the torrent, pitching and yawing like an airliner landing in a cross-wind. But he appeared more in control than before. Or was that just wishful thinking on her part? She bit her bottom lip and prayed.

Wilbur yelled at Jamie to get ready as they closed in on the rock. With spray from the rapids lashing his face, Jamie tightened his grip on one of the piglet's ears, hesitantly let go of the other, then extended his free hand outwards as far as he dared. But shifting his weight like this upset Wilbur's balance, pulling him sideways and onto a course heading straight for the face of the cliff on the far side of the ravine. To make matters worse, this sudden change in direction loosened Jamie's grip on Wilbur's ear, so he instinctively grabbed at the only other means of support available.

'The wings!' Wilbur hollered, panicking. 'For stuffin's sake, don't mess with the wings, man!'

Neither the children nor Wilbur had any way of knowing, of course, that this heart-stopping sequence of events was being masterminded by an evil being who, in the concealment of his lair, was also watching the drama unfold. It appealed to Zorn's twisted sense of humour to see Wilbur's desperate struggle to avoid smashing into the cliff. But for his own devious purposes, he had no intention of letting the piglet or, more importantly, his passenger come to such a sticky end – just yet. With a customary nod towards his cloud 'screen', Zorn caused Wilbur to bank steeply to one side a split second before impact, and returned him on a course aimed directly at the spot where Charlie stood trembling.

Wilbur was beaming from ear to ear. 'Wow, talk about yer legendary flyin' aces! OK, I *knew* I was good,' he crowed, 'but hey, that there manoeuvre surprised even me!'

While Wilbur homed in on the rock, Jamie leaned sideways again, reaching out, his heart in his mouth. Fortunately, his flagging belief in his own ability to succeed against such daunting odds was given a boost by the look in Charlie's eyes, which changed from despair to tail-wagging delight as his young master's face came into focus.

'When I give the command,' yelled Wilbur, 'snatch the pooch! OK, kid?'

'Yes, I – I'm r-ready!'

'OK ... *NOW*!'

But when Jamie's fingers came within a hair's breadth of making contact with Charlie's collar, the little dog disappeared in a puff of green smoke.

In his cavern, Zorn was already holding the terror-stricken dog up by the scruff of the neck, and roaring with laughter as he watched live pictures of Wilbur barrel-rolling crazily this way and that, his dubious aerodynamic qualities made even more suspect by having both of Jamie's arms clamped tightly round his neck.

Wilbur's only concern now was to make it back up to the edge of the ravine before he exhausted what little strength he had left.

'Let go a' my neck!' he shouted at Jamie. 'And start flappin' yer arms! We're badly in need a' some extra lift here!'

It was not, however, any such effort by Jamie that enabled Wilbur to gain the safety of the patch of grass where Susie was standing, but rather Zorn's dastardly intervention. As a result, when the piglet was about to touch down, he also disappeared in a puff of green smoke, leaving Jamie to tumble to earth in an untidy heap.

Relieved though Susie was to have her little brother back in one piece, she was so traumatised by what she had witnessed during the previous few minutes that she was almost stuck for words. 'You OK?' was the best she could offer Jamie by way of comfort as she helped him off the ground.

Jamie's head was in a spin, so it took him a second or two to try and work out where he was and how he had got there. He glanced left, right, up, down and behind, then said, 'Where's Wilbur?'

Glumly, Susie gestured towards the tell-tale smudge of green smoke drifting away over the ravine.

Jamie gazed at it with a look that wavered between puzzlement, sadness and disbelief. ''Sploded?' he asked.

'Just like Charlie did,' Susie nodded

Shaking his head in despair, Jamie lowered his eyes. 'We'll never find Charlie and Jasper now.'

A few moments of muffled sniffling followed, with neither of the children able to speak. Then Susie started to whimper. 'We're doomed, Jamie. We'll never see Mummy again – ever.'

* * * * *

– CHAPTER ELEVEN –

SHORTLY AFTERWARDS –
OVERLOOKING THE RAVINE

The stark reality of Susie's words of woe was all it took to drain away the last dregs of fortitude that had kept Jamie going through all the setbacks he and his sister had suffered since setting out on their quest to rescue his pet mouse. He started to cry as well.

They slumped down side-by-side on the grass, feeling lost, far from home, with no way of getting back.

Then, out of the blue, they heard a man's voice calling them. 'Come now, children,' he said, 'don't be sad.' But there was something about the voice that didn't strike them as being particularly sympathetic: something quite eerie and sinister, with a hollow ring that seemed chillingly familiar.

The children's attention was drawn towards the other side of the ravine, where a large, glowing sphere had appeared, hovering as if by magic in front of the cliff. On it was projected the image of a man: an evil-looking man, with horns sprouting from his head and a sneering grin on his face.

'It's him!' Susie hissed. 'Him that took Jasper!'

'That's right, little girl,' Zorn smirked, 'but no need to worry about your animals any more.' He showed them Jasper dangling by his tail from one hand, and Charlie hanging by his collar from the other. 'As you can see, they are quite safe with me.' He glared at each terrified pet in turn, then licked his lips before muttering, 'For the moment, that is.'

'Leave them alone!' Jamie shouted. 'Give them back – now!'

Zorn assumed an air of mock compassion. 'Of course, of course, sonny boy. And I'll even make it easy for you to come and get them. Look...' He popped his fingers and a flimsy rope bridge materialised in front of the children, spanning the ravine and leading to what appeared to be the mouth of a tunnel in the cliff face opposite. On the luminous sphere, Zorn held Charlie and Jasper aloft again. 'Come and get them, kiddywinkies,' he teased. 'They will be in there waiting for you.' With that, he threw his head back and laughed, his voice echoing through the gorge as his image grew fainter and fainter, until finally evaporating in a mushroom of green smoke.

The children were more confused and frightened than ever now. They looked over to the tunnel where Zorn had said their pets were being held, then down at the torrent, foaming and tumbling over its rocky bed far below. Finally, they looked at the rope bridge with its rickety deck of slatted wooden planks.

'*I'*m not going over that,' said Susie, adding that the very thought gave her goose pimples.

Jamie, on the other hand, was willing himself *not* to think about it. 'We've got to save Charlie and Jasper, Susie. And don't worry, I'll go first.' He set his jaw, reached up and grabbed a rope handrail, then stepped onto the threshold of the bridge. 'It's all right, Susie, follow me!'

But Susie didn't share her brother's daredevil attitude, nor, indeed, his optimism. She shook her head vigorously. 'No, no, no, no, *no*! I could never walk on that wobbly thing. *Never*!'

Meanwhile, young Mungo was leading Maggie towards a glimmer of daylight that had appeared at a bend in the tunnel up ahead. Maggie was still adamant that the screams she had heard earlier were that of a child, and, in her considered opinion, the child in question was one of hers. She tapped Mungo on the shoulder and stopped, listening carefully again.

'Can you hear that?' she said. 'It's like a waterfall or something.'

Mungo stood in silence for a moment, then nodded his head. 'Yes indeed, mistress – a mere murmur, but a waterfall it would seem to be. And coming from the direction of that glow yonder.'

Suddenly, what sounded like the shouts of a young boy rang out over the distant babble of cascading water.

Maggie caught her breath. 'Jamie!' she gasped, then brushed past Mungo and pressed on through the gloom towards the light at the bend in the tunnel.

By this time, Jamie, although feeling much more

afraid than he had led his sister to believe, was almost half way across the bridge, stepping cautiously over the gaps between its wooden slats. He paused and called over his shoulder: 'Come on, Susie! It's n-not d-dangerous!'

Susie had now managed to pluck up enough courage to grasp the end of one of the rope handrails, but kept her feet planted safely on terra firma. She glanced at the void between the bridge and the angry waters thundering over the bottom of the ravine, and felt physically sick.

'Don't look down!' Jamie shouted. 'Just come over with your eyes shut!'

Not for the first time, prevailing circumstances prevented Susie from telling her little brother precisely what he could do with his silly advice. All the same, she didn't relish the thought of being left alone on this side of the ravine, so maybe there was something in what he had suggested after all. And the more she thought about it, the more obvious it became that there really wasn't any choice. She duly closed her eyes, gritted her teeth and moved hesitantly onto the bridge. But her new-found courage was short-lived. After taking just two steps, she froze – petrified, unable to move an inch, forward or back.

'H-E-E-E-LP!' she wailed. 'Come and get me, Jamie! I'm stuck!'

Jamie, however, had troubles enough of his own to contend with. The bridge had now started to swing and shake every time he took a step, so to steady himself he was forced to keep grabbing for one of the suspension ropes that ran down at regular intervals from the handrails to either side of the deck. Despite having warned Susie not to look down, he was finding it well nigh impossible to follow his own advice. Some of the gaps between the slats were wide enough to allow a child's foot to slip through, so failing to watch where he put his own feet would be a recipe for disaster. And the roar of the rapids rising from the bottom of the gorge served as a constant reminder. But what he hadn't bargained for was the state of the bridge becoming progressively more dilapidated the farther across he ventured. (Zorn, true to his scheming ways, was seeing to that!). Still, Jamie had made his mind up and there was no going back now. He braced himself and gently eased a foot over the next gap. Then the very thing he had been trying hardest *not* to think about actually happened...

'*H-E-E-E-LP!*' he yelled, as the rotting plank he was standing on gave way. 'Save me, Susie! I'm falling!'

Susie found herself looking on in horror as Jamie's leg dropped through the floor of the bridge, throwing him sideways and wrenching his fingers away from the rope he had been holding onto. He was now hanging head-first over the side of the bridge, clinging to one end of the broken plank and staring directly into the stomach-churning chasm of the gorge. His only hope of avoiding certain death rested on having the strength to haul himself back up, but the harder he tried, the more the bridge swung and shook. (Zorn was also seeing to that!).

If Jamie had been granted a wish right then,

it would have been for Wilbur the flying piglet to make another appearance – and the sooner the better. The trouble was that he didn't even have a hand free to dip into his pocket for the magic coins. He felt his grip weaken and he started to slip. But just when he thought all was lost, he heard Susie's voice, weepy and trembly, but heartening all the same…

'Don't panic, Jamie. I – I'll help you.'

Out of the corner of his eye, Jamie could just make out his sister's feet appearing and disappearing between the slats as the bridge swayed first one way then the other. Her feet were moving very slowly, but they were moving, and towards him at that. Of a sudden, he had hope – not much, perhaps, but enough to give him strength.

The harsh fact of the matter was, however, that both children were now exactly where Zorn wanted, and it would take more than a ray of hope to keep them from the fate he had planned. As if to prove it, the moment Jamie renewed his struggle to heave himself back onto the deck of the bridge, it dipped towards him, and he felt himself starting to slip once more.

The same sudden movement had also thrown Susie off balance, and she stood holding on grimly to one of the handrails, afraid to move a muscle, her eyes tightly closed again. It was only when she heard a familiar voice calling her name that she dared open them. At first she had thought she was hearing things; now she wondered if her eyes were deceiving her, tricked by the same cruel magic that she and her brother had been tormented by since falling into that horrible pit.

'Mummy?' she whispered, her chin quivering. Could that *really* be her? It seemed too good to be true. Susie blinked away the tears that had been misting her eyes and focussed hard on the shadowed face of a woman who had appeared at the far side of the bridge. And it was true. It really was her mother.

Maggie was standing in the mouth of the tunnel, relieved beyond belief to have found her children at last, but horrified to see the awful danger they were in. 'Susie,' she shouted again, 'don't worry. I'm here now. Everything's going to be fine.'

Susie felt her spirits rise for the first time since embarking on this madcap venture. 'Oh, Mummy, Mummy!' she called out. 'Help us! It's Jamie – he's falling!'

'It's OK, Susie – it's OK. And hold on, Jamie. I'm coming.'

Her confidence thus bolstered, Susie began to inch her way across the bridge again. 'And – and, Mummy,' she blurted out, 'the bad man who stole Jasper – he's got Charlie now as well, and – and –'

'It's all right, Susie – calm down – I'm coming to get you.' Maggie stepped falteringly onto the bridge, then glanced at the fearsome drop beneath her feet. Her blood ran cold. She knew that her dread of heights was a phobia shared by her children, so could fully empathise with their present state of terror.

Young Mungo emerged from the tunnel behind Maggie and took but a moment to appraise the situation. 'Zorn!' he growled. 'Only he would treat defenceless children in such a vile way.' He stepped forward and gripped Maggie's arm. 'No, Mistress McKim, please go no further. I fear you could make matters worse – *if* this is what I think it is.'

'*IF*? There are no ifs about it! Those are *my* children out there!'

'Please, leave this to me.' Mungo pulled Maggie back, then positioned himself in front of her, facing the bridge and barring her way. He immediately assumed his wizardly pose, eyes closed, the splayed fingers of one hand pointing across the ravine. '*Oh-h-h, ooblan, ooblan, ooblan...*,' he droned.

But before Mungo could complete his incantation, a howl from Jamie gave stark notice that his grip was finally about to give out. Maggie could only look on helplessly as he slipped further and further over the side of the bridge. Then, just as it seemed he was about to plunge headlong into the gorge, he managed to hook an arm round one of the suspension ropes, which halted his fall, but left him dangling in mid air. Maggie realised that her little boy would be unable to hold on like this for long. Frantically, she thumped Mungo's back with her fist. 'Don't just stand there talking gibberish! *Do*, something!'

'You *must* trust me,' Mungo came back. 'What you see before you is a product of Zorn's sorcery, and the only way to reverse it is by countering it with my own – the good versus the bad.' Closing his ears to Maggie's pleas, he resumed his incantation, ending in a full-blooded roar of '*TERMINABO-O-OH*!'. But when he re-opened his eyes, nothing had changed.

'Useless, as usual!' Maggie snapped. 'Now, get out of my way!'

Undeterred, Mungo stood firm and began to repeat the same magic words, leaving Maggie to vent her frustrations to the back of his head.

While all this was going on, Susie had kept edging across the bridge and was now standing directly above Jamie, with both of her hands clamped firmly to the handrail.

'Oh, Susie,' Jamie wailed, 'help me, please. I – I don't want to die.'

Susie was trembling with fear, but knew her little brother's life depended on her being brave. She sniffed away her tears and knelt down, gingerly extending one of her hands towards him.

Over at the mouth of the tunnel, Mungo was still doggedly reciting his spell, though tell-tale beads of sweat were beginning to show on his brow. His struggles to overcome the trials already encountered on this mission of mercy had taken their toll.

In his lair, Zorn had continued to watch developments on his cloud 'screen' and was now gloating over Mungo's deteriorating condition. 'Go on, you fool, keep using up your precious Power,' he snarled. 'The less you have, the quicker you will perish at my feet – which will be very soon now.'

He rose from his throne and, silencing the blare of heavy metal music with a sweep of his arm, commanded the swarms of Keelies on the cavern floor to cease their revelling and prepare to witness the righting of the greatest wrong ever to blight their mystic order. 'At long last,' he declared, 'I, Zorn, will prove beyond doubt that I am the true Master, and the title of Great High Sorcerer will finally be mine … *MINE*!'

The mob of malicious goblins bayed their approval, which Zorn acknowledged by striking a pose of puffed-up, chin-jutting arrogance. When he had drunk his fill of the Keelies' adulation, he raised a hand and directed their attention upwards to the 'screen' and its live images of the drama now unfolding on the bridge. 'But before the commencement of the great event,' he boomed, 'let us take time to enjoy together the conclusion of my amusing little sideshow…'

Susie was on her knees, leaning over the side of the bridge, reaching out for Jamie, when the deck beneath her gave a sudden lurch. She screamed for her life as she felt herself slip, but instinctively grabbed the same rope that Jamie's arm was hooked around. The deck lurched again, accompanied by an ominous creaking noise.

'Look!' Maggie shouted at Mungo. 'The bridge – it's collapsing!' She thumped his back again. 'Let me past! My children – they're going to be killed!'

Mungo turned and held Maggie by the shoulders. He stared into her eyes with the same hypnotic look that had lulled her into trusting him at the start of this bizarre trip. 'Believe me,' he murmured, 'there is only one way … *the* way.'

Though determined not to fall under Mungo's spell again, Maggie felt her resistance begin to waver. A tear trickled down her cheek as she implored him to let her go to her children. 'Please,' she said, 'Susie and Jamie are all I've got now.'

A steely look came to Mungo's eyes and, without saying a word, he turned to face the bridge once more. Standing squarely in Maggie's path, he stared heavenward for a moment, then readied himself in the now-familiar way. '*Oh, ooblan, ooblan,*,' he began afresh, '*Oh, ooblan, ooblan, ooblan…*

But, as much as Mungo may have thought he had succeeded in curbing Maggie's impatience, he soon found out that she wasn't about to let him waste time repeating a ritual she feared would produce the same fumbled results as before. On top of that, the heart-rending sound of Susie and Jamie screaming had become more than she could endure. She gave Mungo's back an almighty shove. 'Out of my way! OUT. OF. MY. WAY!'

Yet, weakened as he was, an overpowering need to counter Zorn's black magic lent Mungo the strength to stand firm and the determination to complete his spell. '*Ooblan repetabo verum!*' he chanted, before inhaling deeply and shouting, '*TERMINABO TORMENTU-U-U-M!*'

But when he opened his eyes, still nothing had changed, until a sudden darkening of the sky and a rumbling thunderclap heralded the onset of a storm, which blasted through the ravine and set the rope bridge swinging more violently than ever.

'Look what your mumbo-jumbo has done now!' Maggie hollered. 'My children! They'll be blown off the bridge!'

Mungo raised his eyes heavenward again, his chest heaving, his fists clenched. 'I defy your evil sorcery!' he yelled into the howling of the wind. 'And in the name of all that is good, I command you, Zorn, to release the children from this nightmare – NOW!'

'Your wish is my command,' Zorn sneered. 'But for you, milksop, the *real* nightmare is only beginning.' With his green eyes blazing, he glared at the cloud 'screen', then bellowed triumphantly, 'THE TIME HAS COME ... DELIVER THE MORTAL BRATS!'

A bolt of lightning smashed into the cliff top on the opposite side of the ravine from Maggie, destroying the bridge's anchoring blocks in an explosion of rubble. She could do nothing but gasp in horror as the bridge fell away, dislodging the children, who plummeted into a huge, vaporous whirlpool that had appeared beneath them. Maggie buried her face against Mungo's back, unable to watch Susie and Jamie being hurled round and round, drawn ever downward, their arms and legs flailing, their screams inaudible against the roaring of the storm.

Mungo looked with disgust at the hellish scene he believed to be the latest manifestation of Zorn's barbarity, then turned to face Maggie. 'Trust me,' he said, 'it may not be as it seems.'

For once, Maggie was so utterly devastated by what had happened that she had neither the inclination to argue nor the will to resist.

Mungo took her hand and shepherded her back

into the tunnel. 'Come, mistress, we do not have much further to travel … *if* this is what I think it is.'

* * * * *

– CHAPTER TWELVE –

MOMENTS LATER –
ZORN'S SUBTERRANEAN LAIR...

A swirling cone of mist penetrated the roof of the cavern, its accompanying wind buffeting Zorn's mob of evil goblins as it descended towards them. Then, suddenly, the vortex evaporated, leaving a bewildered Susie and Jamie lying dazed and dizzy on the cavern floor.

'Welcome to the abode of Zorn, Lord of Goblin Hall!' one of the mob shouted. 'Otherwise known as the Gateway to Hell!' another called out, triggering an outburst of high-pitched sniggering and tittering that had the children thinking for a moment that they had been transported into the hyenas' enclosure at a zoo. But there was never a zoo like this...

Even that awful dragons' den they had fallen into hadn't smelled as foul. There was a stench of rotten eggs and coal smoke, mixed with the nauseating whiff of stale sweat radiating from every Keelie who came close. And the walls oozing slime. And the eerie green light that cast shadows into corners where cowed wretches draped in sackcloth lurked and moaned like zombies. And the pervading thrum of a pipe organ. Not the uplifting strains the children had been accustomed to hearing in their father's church, but heavy, doleful chords that added an extra note of doom to this soul-destroying scene.

Yet it was the presence of the Keelies themselves that troubled the children more than anything. Old Mungo had given them a fairly detailed description of these villains of the goblin world, but that hadn't prepared them for the shock of being propelled into a living, breathing crowd of them. Although small, the Keelies were stocky, muscular little devils, brutish in demeanour, with faces like grotesquely-carved pumpkins, and a shifty look in their eyes.

Zorn stood gazing down from his dais, savouring the sight of his minions catcalling and laughing while they milled round the children – prodding them, grabbing them, roughly hauling them to their feet.

'Excellent!' he said to himself. 'The bait is finally in my trap!'

A group of Keelies bundled Susie and Jamie across the floor and onto the dais, where Zorn was waiting beside a large cage suspended from the ceiling by a chain looped through a system of cog wheels. Inside the cage hung two smaller cages, one containing Charlie the dog, the other Jasper, Jamie's white mouse.

'Throw the brats in with their animals!' Zorn growled.

The Keelies did his bidding, then took hold of the chain and hauled away until the cage was several metres above the floor.

'Go on, kiddywinkies,' Zorn guffawed as Susie and Jamie screamed in terror, 'bawl your heads off. It will bring that fool Mungo to me all the sooner.'

He was right. Back in the tunnel, Maggie heard her children's cries and was jolted from the numbing sense of grief that had overcome her after she'd seen them plunge from the bridge.

Mungo urged her onwards. 'Take heart and believe in the good, Mistress McKim. You will soon have your children with you again … just as I always knew you would.'

Although Susie and Jamie were beside themselves with fear, they derived some comfort from being reunited with their pets, albeit that they were now in the same desperate situation themselves. And it was about to get even worse.

'Did I not tell you that your stupid creatures would be safe with me?' Zorn sneered. 'Well, enjoy their company while you can – which will not be for long!'

He snapped his fingers and a large hole appeared in the floor beneath the cage. Deep within it a fire was burning fiercely. Zorn then nodded towards the cog wheels, which clicked into motion as the supporting chain began to lower the cage link-by-link towards the fiery pit.

As soon as Susie and Jamie realised what was happening, they tugged frantically at the bars of the cage. But their pleas for mercy were only mocked by Zorn and his attendant Keelies, while the crowds on the floor whooped and cheered.

Suddenly, Zorn spun round and pointed at the entrance to a tunnel on the opposite side of the cavern.

'SILENCE!' he shouted.

All that could be heard now was the children's whimpering and the clicking of cogs as the cage inched relentlessly downward. A self-satisfied smirk came to Zorn's lips. 'So,' he murmured, 'the gallant saviour is about to grace us with his presence … at last!'

A moment later, young Mungo and Maggie appeared at the mouth the tunnel, where they paused to allow their eyes to become accustomed to the light. As they peered out over a sea of hostile Keelie faces, Mungo's expression remained deliberately inscrutable, but Maggie's changed from bewilderment to one of shock the instant she saw her children. Without thinking, she made to rush towards them.

This was precisely what Zorn wanted. He nodded in her direction, causing her to career into an invisible force field he had placed in her path. She staggered backwards, holding her head.

Satisfied that all was going as planned, Zorn stepped swaggering from his dais. 'Surely you did not think I would make it easy for you,' he called out to Mungo.

But Mungo was too concerned about Maggie's immediate well-being to respond. Only when he was satisfied that she had only been stunned did he motion her to stand back and allow him to take charge of the situation. By now, Zorn had positioned himself in the centre of the cavern, facing Mungo, a smug look on his face, legs apart, arms akimbo.

Chattering excitedly, Zorn's hordes of followers made way for the impending showdown by shuffling off to either side. Meanwhile, the cage in which the children were trapped continued its slow but relentless descent towards the burning abyss.

'Oh, Mummy, Mummy, come and help us!' Susie shouted when she caught sight of her mother.

'And hurry!' Jamie yelled. 'We're going to be roasted!'

As Maggie stood struggling to clear her head, young Mungo strode forward and slapped the palm of his hand against the invisible barrier.

Zorn gave a mocking laugh. 'It will take more than that to move it, *Great* High Sorcerer. So then, let's see what you can do!'

Foregoing his usual preliminaries, Mungo took a pace back, then pointed the spread fingers of one hand at the force field. *'Aperando zibanno!'* he shouted. Instantly, jets of fire shot from his fingertips and bounced off the barrier like the blast from a flame thrower cashing into a concrete wall.

Maggie cringed behind him, her arm raised against the heat.

'Aperando!' he shouted again, but still his bombardment rebounded.

'Use your precious Power,' Zorn taunted. 'Go on, Mungo! More! More!'

'APERANDO!' Mungo repeated, louder and more vigorously. But the force field still held firm. Without the aid of the Great High Sorcerer's staff,

which had been broken in two by Zorn during their last encounter many centuries before, Mungo was unable to summon the full force of the Power. To make matters worse, his limited strength had been further depleted by striving to overcome the other obstacles placed in his way since being duped into entering Zorn's underground domain. Mungo began to sweat profusely, while the children's screams continued to torment his ears.

Zorn pointed at their cage, laughing. 'The mortal brats, Mungo! Look! They need your wonderful *Power* to rescue them!'

Maggie had now recovered sufficiently from the blow to her head to focus more clearly on the grim reality of what was happening.

The children called out to her again

'Let them go!' she yelled at Zorn. 'Please, I *beg* you!'

But Zorn had other ideas.

The jets of flame from Mungo's fingers had now begun to falter, firing in irregular spurts as he dropped to his knees, gasping for breath.

Zorn was enjoying this. Buoyed up by the cheering of his Keelie thugs, he revelled in the spectacle of young Mungo's unequal struggle for a few more moments, then snapped his fingers. What looked like a shimmering heat haze rose momentarily in front of Mungo as the force field dissolved into thin air.

Zorn stared disdainfully down at him. 'See how easy it is, Mungo ... for someone who has what it takes?'

A scornful frown was all Mungo had the strength to muster by way of reply.

Realising that the barrier had gone, Maggie lunged forward in a desperate attempt to reach her children. But as she tried to find a way past Zorn, he took her by the arm, pulling her to him.

From a distance, Maggie had thought Zorn to be an ordinary man done up in some weird sort of Halloween costume. Close up, however, she could see that every grotesque detail about him was real – from the reptilian scaliness of his skin to the horns sprouting from his skull; the slitty, cat-like pupils of his eyes; his yellow, pointed teeth; and, most revolting of all, his breath, which Maggie thought smelled like a blocked drain.

She started to thump his chest with her fists. 'Let go of me! Please ... *please*, let me go to my children!'

But Maggie's blows were but the beating of butterfly wings to Zorn. She felt her flesh creep as he grabbed her wrists and leered down at her.

'So, a spirited one, hmm? How perfect! Oh yes indeed, my beauty, I will look forward to dealing with *you* later!' With a shout of, 'Restrain her!', he hurled her bodily towards the nearest bunch of Keelies.

Maggie fought them off as best she could, but even though the Keelies were barely up to her knees in height, she was no match for their strength in numbers.

'Take her and prepare her!' Zorn barked. 'You know what to do!'

Susie and Jamie looked on, horror-struck and helpless, as their mother was hustled away through the crowds of baying Keelies. And all the while their cage clicked steadily down towards the fiery pit.

Mungo was now making a supreme effort to get

back on his feet. 'Let her go, Zorn,' he panted. 'And – and the children. This is not their concern.'

'Ah, but you forget, Mungo, that without the mortal brats and their silly mouse, I could never have tempted you to come here.' Zorn gave an evil chuckle. 'The least I can do now is arrange a barbecue for them, no?' He placed a foot on Mungo's chest and shoved him onto his backside. 'I have waited a thousand years to take my revenge, and this time you do not have an old man to save you with his *magic* stick.' Zorn reached round and pulled a length of carved wood from his belt. 'And here is the half of that very stick which, as you may well recall, I snatched from your beloved Master when he condemned me to what he referred to as the infernal depths of hell.' Zorn threw the stick at Mungo. 'Well, it is now your turn to be cast into the abyss, and you can take your useless piece of firewood with you!'

Mungo stared at the stick for a few seconds, then picked it up and glowered at Zorn. 'Not only did you debase our creed by breaking the sacred icon bequeathed to us by the Mighty One on high, you also –'

'Spare me that bunkum!' Zorn cut in. 'The only thing I did by snapping that pathetic twig in two was to deprive *you* of its Power! You, the so-called successor of the old duffer you called the Master!' Zorn puffed out his chest and beat it with his fist. 'Well, *I*, the true Master, do not need such a crutch. And the only thing that piece of kindling will help you do now is burn! BURN!'

With his eyes staring crazily, Zorn pointed a finger

at the floor in front of Mungo. *'Aperando turbabbo*!' he yelled. In an instant, a whirlwind enveloped Mungo and swept him upwards. Zorn then turned and nodded in the direction of his dais. A peal of thunder reverberated round the cavern as the whirlwind materialised inside the cage containing the children, who cringed terrified against its bars while the swirling vortex dispersed to leave Mungo lying motionless at their feet.

Zorn acknowledged the cheering of his onlooking minions with lordly gestures as he strutted back towards the dais. 'For *your* time has come to feel the lick of the flames in the dungeons of hell,' he shouted at Mungo, 'while I, Zorn, take my rightful place at last as Great High Sorcerer in the mortal world above. Yes! And the power of *my* Mighty One, the Prince of Darkness, will finally be unleashed without restraint!'

He climbed onto his dais, where, striking a suitably imperious pose, he addressed the crowds of fawning Keelies gazing up at him from the floor.

'Bow before your lord!' he boomed.

As one, the gathering of evil goblins dipped their heads.

With a demented glint in his eye, Zorn now turned to Scurvo and Tentor, the most grovelling of his Keelie subjects, who were standing close by, patiently awaiting his pleasure. 'The moment is nigh!' he snarled. 'Fetch the regalia!'

While the toadying twosome scuttled off tugging their forelocks, Zorn moved to the centre of the dais and positioned himself behind his throne. He closed his eyes, raised his arms and began to deliver a pledge of loyalty to the Devil. As the wailing of a ghostly choir swelled over the drone of organ music, a green mist rose up to enshroud the throne. Then, with the final words of Zorn's pledge still echoing round the chamber, the mist cleared to reveal that the throne had been replaced by a long, stone altar, inscribed with weird occult symbols.

Inside the cage, Susie and Jamie were becoming more and more distressed. They stared at young Mungo, lying on the sparred floor in front of them and clearly still suffering the after-effects of his latest mugging by Zorn.

'Look at that stick in his hand,' Susie hissed in her brother's ear. 'Just like the one old Mungo showed us.'

'And his long frock thingy as well,' Jamie added, '– just like old Mungo's.'

'That's right. And why was he in that tunnel with our Mummy anyway?'

As the cage took yet another downwards jerk, Jamie decided that, suspicious as he was of this stranger, bold measures were called for. He gave Mungo a prod with his foot. 'Get up, mister, whoever you are. And help us quick. We're going to be barbie-coo'd, and so are you!'

Young Mungo blinked at him. 'Master Jamie? Wh-what are you doing here?' Then he noticed Susie. 'And little Miss Susie too? Where – where *are* we?'

'How do you know who we are?' Jamie frowned.

'Yes,' said Susie, 'and what are you doing wearing old Mungo's night shirt?'

'Why, because – because I am he. Do you not recognise me?'

'No,' said Jamie, his frown deepening. 'And why did the bad man throw a piece of stick like old Mungo's at you?'

'And why did he call *you* Mungo?' Susie added.

'Stick? Bad man? What bad man?' Young Mungo rubbed his forehead. 'I – I can't seem to think clearly.'

'*That* stick,' Susie pressed. 'The one in your hand. Why is it like old Mungo's?'

While Mungo stared in bewilderment at the piece of wood, the Keelies on the cavern floor began to clap their hands slowly as Maggie, dressed in a long white robe, was led trance-like through their midst towards the dais.

Seeing their mother, Susie and Jamie flung themselves against the bars of the cage and called frantically to her again. But Maggie appeared unaware that they were there, or even where she was herself.

Scurvo and Tentor now returned to the dais carrying an array of ceremonial trappings. As they approached the altar, Zorn stripped himself to the waist, revealing a torso covered in grey, wolf-like hair. Scurvo presented him with armbands fashioned from intertwined serpents, and a matching chain with a pendant in the form of a human skull. Tentor then handed him a hooded black cape. All of these items were embellished with the same mysterious insignia that had been carved into the stone of the altar.

A sense of expectancy was rapidly developing within the ranks of Keelie onlookers, who elbowed each other and mumbled excitedly while the wailing of the ghostly choir grew louder. Lightning flickered and thunder rumbled through the cavern as Zorn prepared to don the black cape. He was now so absorbed in the drama of the evolving ritual that he had become completely unmindful of what was happening inside the cage...

Young Mungo was gradually regaining his senses. He looked at the children, then glanced down into the fiery chasm, and the awful gravity of the situation began to strike home. It was only then that it dawned on him why the children had wondered why he had 'a stick like old Mungo's' in his hand. He peered at it, taking but a moment to realise that what Zorn had thrown at him truly was one half of the Great High Sorcerer's sacred staff. Without wasting another second, he reached into a fold of his robe and brought out the other half, which, though unknown to Zorn, he had kept steadfastly by his side since their last confrontation a thousand years earlier. With trembling hands, he readied himself to reunite one segment of the sacred relic with the other.

Maggie, her eyes glazed and unblinking, was now slowly ascending the steps to the dais, goaded onwards by prodding Keelie fingers. Zorn eyed her admiringly as she made her way to the altar, where she halted and stood transfixed. Staring up at her, the congregation of malicious goblins began to grunt in a ponderous, rhythmic monotone. Zorn now lifted the hood of his cape over his head, so that only the green gleam of his eyes and the cruel twist of his mouth were visible beneath its shadow. He drew a dagger from a scabbard offered up by one of his lackeys, cautiously ran a finger over its tip, then, with a smirk of satisfaction, laid it on the altar.

All the while, the cage inched ever lower. Desperately, Mungo prayed a silent prayer to the Mighty One on high. He asked to be granted a second chance to access those vital elements of the Power he had so recently drawn from the Lightning Tree, but had drained away in attempting to overcome the challenges cunningly set by Zorn. While Mungo prayed, he brought together and enclosed in his fist the severed ends of the ancient staff. Being granted the ability to make it whole again would be the only hope, not just for his own survival and that of Maggie and her children, but for the future welfare of the entire mortal world as well.

'Lend me the Power!' he pleaded aloud. 'I implore you, oh Mighty One, who resides unseen but all-seeing in the Higher Place, to afford me the mystic energies of the Lightning Tree – just one more time!'

Susie nudged her little brother. 'The Lightning Tree! He knows about it!'

'Maybe needs to charge up his battery,' Jamie ventured, 'like old Mungo told us *he* could do.'

'Yes, and – and he had that piece of stick in his nightshirt, just like old Mungo did.' Susie shook her head. 'I don't understand. Unless – unless it means he maybe *is* old Mungo after all!'

The bottom of the cage was now almost level

with the floor of the dais, with the heat and smoke from the subterranean inferno becoming more intense with every click of the chain. Anxiously, Mungo opened his fist, only to find that the two ends of the staff had not fused together. He swiftly wrapped his fingers round the break and repeated his silent prayer.

A few metres away, Zorn was still gazing approvingly at Maggie as he motioned her to lie down on the altar. She obeyed without resistance, while in the background, the wailing of the ghostly choir and the throb of the Keelies' grunting grew steadily louder.

In the cage, young Mungo opened his hand to expose once more the abutting ends of the sacred staff, but, to his dismay, they still had not bonded. It was degrading enough to have been publicly belittled by Zorn, but having his entreaties ignored by the Mighty One himself amounted to the worst humiliation imaginable. Mungo lowered his head in shame, knowing full well that the rules of the Brotherhood stated that only once in all the centuries of his life could a wizard avail himself of the Lightning Tree's magical properties in the way he had done before setting out on this mission. Now, thanks to Zorn's guile, that well-meant undertaking had turned out to be nothing but a fool's errand – and promising the most horrific of consequences to boot.

Mungo glanced at the children, then cast his eyes in Maggie's direction, and the thought of what was about to befall these innocent people filled him with remorse for letting himself be tricked into having them used as pawns in Zorn's despicable game. He stood with his shoulders hunched, a picture of dejection. Throughout his long life, Mungo had stressed to others the importance of believing in the good and denying the bad, yet now it seemed the forces of good were about to forsake their most devout defender.

Or were they...?

Out of Mungo's line of vision, a dark shape fluttered furtively from the shadows and settled on a ledge above the dais.

Susie spotted it. 'Look there, Jamie! Is that a ... *bat*?'

'No – think it's just a bird,' Jamie assured her.

'*Algaboorabba*!' cawed the bird.

'Old Mungo's blackbird!' gasped Jamie.

'*Algaboorabba*!' cawed the bird again, and swooped onto the top of the cage. '*Magic money, boy – him*! *Magic money – him*!'

This confused Jamie. 'Money? Him? Who's him?'

'*Silly bugger*!' said the bird, then indicated Mungo with a squawk and some rapid jabbing of his beak.

'Do as he says!' Susie snapped. 'And be quick about it!'

With his head still crowded with memories of all the nightmares they'd lived through in the past few hours, Jamie had almost forgotten about the two gold coins the young jackdaw had given him back at the entrance to the underground passage: the coins that had enabled them to conjure up Wilbur the flying piglet to try and help rescue Charlie from that raging torrent. Jamie started to rummage in his pockets.

'Hurry up!' Susie yelled. 'We're running out of time!'

Precious seconds of mumbling and fumbling later, Jamie succeeded in producing the coins, which Susie swiftly grabbed. With a cry of, 'Here! Wake up and *do* something!' she thrust them into young Mungo's hand.

But Mungo seemed too lost in his cloud of self-reproach to have taken any notice.

And the cage jerked inexorably downward into the mouth of the flaming chasm.

Over on the altar, Maggie was now lying flat on her back, her eyes closed, her expression serene, while around her all hell was about to break loose.

Zorn had been watching her every move with a smile of wicked intent on his lips, but suddenly, he raised his head and spun round to face the rough stone wall behind the dais. 'Hear me, Almighty Lucifer!' he bellowed. 'Behold, I bring you a gift – a token of my loyalty!'

Lightning danced and thunder growled while an eerie red glow began to develop on the surface of the wall. Within it there appeared the blurred image of a head: a hideous, horned head; half man, half beast; several metres high, with a face wearing a vicious look resembling Zorn's, but with eyes and mouth more vicious still. It was the face of evil personified. The face of the Devil himself.

As the image became sharper, a host of demons could be seen swarming around it in a garland of flames. These skinny sentinels of the gates to hell were so repulsive in their nakedness that they made the Keelies look almost cherub-like in comparison. They had talons for fingers, fang-filled mouths fixed in sneering grins, and long rats' tails tipped with poison arrow heads.

'All hail the Prince of Darkness!' boomed Zorn, and the Keelie throngs brayed in unison while sinking awe-struck to their knees. In the background, the discordant strains of organ and phantom choir rose to an ear-piercing crescendo.

And this was what it took to stir young Mungo from his stupor – this and the heat of the coins as they began to glow in the palm of his hand. Then he noticed the young jackdaw bobbing impatiently up and down on top of the cage. 'It's Jake!' he said, squinting through the smoke. 'And – and you brought me the magic coins!'

'*Clever boy!*' croaked Jake, and promptly flew off, mission accomplished.

For Mungo, though, the final and most testing phase of his own mission was only just beginning. And he knew it. But there was a more optimistic set to his expression as he once again wrapped his fingers round the two halves of the staff – this time pressing the gold coins firmly against the break.

The bottom of the cage was now below the floor of the dais, and still descending. While Mungo mouthed his silent prayer once more, the children clung to each other, trembling. Both were wishing their father would appear to save them, just as he'd always done before: like the time Susie got stuck up an apple tree in the garden, or when Jamie got his head wedged between the bars of the front gate. And he would never have let that bad man over there hurt Mummy – ever. But Daddy was in heaven now, and wherever that might be, it was far, far away from this terrible place. They looked up at the small cages that held their panic-stricken pets and tried their best to comfort them with soothing words. But the little creatures could see and hear nothing now but the raging inferno that waited to devour them all.

Zorn, for his part, was still oblivious to everything except the image of the Devil projected on the cavern wall, and the ritual he was about to perform in his honour. With a sweep of his arm, he directed the Devil's attention to Maggie, lying comatose on the altar.

'See, sire!' he called out. 'A bride! I bring you a mortal bride!'

A sinister smile played at the corners of the Devil's mouth as he ran his eyes over Zorn's sacrificial offering. 'HER SOUL!' he roared, in a voice so chilling it sounded as though it were rising from a cold, empty grave. 'GIVE ME HER SOUL!'

While his Keelie thugs howled like wolves under a full moon, Zorn turned to face the altar and ran a claw-like finger down Maggie's cheek, allowing it to linger for a moment at her throat. With slow, deliberate movements, he lifted the sacrificial dagger, stepped back and paused to survey his victim with eyes radiating a weird mix of menace and fascination. A hush descended upon the Keelie congregation as he commenced the delivery of a solemn oath...

'With this blade, forged in the flames of hell, and

from whose thrust no living body can survive, I convey the soul of this mortal creature to our Lord Lucifer, the almighty Prince of Darkness.'

Zorn then threw his cloak open and raised the knife above his head, its point aimed at Maggie's heart.

* * * * *

– CHAPTER THIRTEEN –

A MOMENT LATER...

A new glow of self-confidence spread across Mungo's face as he opened his hand and regarded the ancient staff, its halves now firmly bonded by a gleaming band of gold. The magical properties of the Power had been restored at last! With a beam of white heat shooting from the end of the staff, he cut an opening in the side of the cage and quickly helped Susie and Jamie through. He then clambered out himself and aimed the staff at Zorn's back, just as he was about to plunge the dagger into Maggie's chest.

'ENOUGH!' he shouted.

Startled, Zorn spun round and was astounded to see Mungo standing there, bright-eyed, straight-backed and self-assured, the very opposite of the broken man he had been just a few minutes earlier. 'What cheap trickery is this?' Zorn rasped. Then he noticed the staff in Mungo's hand, and realised that, by whatever obscure means it had become whole again, the threat it posed might just be real, so had to be quashed – immediately.

There was a hint of desperation about him as he prepared to hurl the sacrificial dagger at Mungo, who knocked it from his hand with another blazing flash from the tip of the staff.

'Well, Zorn,' he said through a wry smile, 'who has what it takes now?'

Zorn was unable to contain his anger at having his supremacy questioned, particularly in front of his Keelie subjects, and even worse, with the Devil himself as witness. He glared at Mungo, raised his hand and fired a bolt of lightning, which Mungo swatted like a fly and reduced to a hissing puff of of steam.

'Do your worst, Zorn,' he taunted. 'Oh yes, you showed yourself to be very brave when it came to bullying defenceless mortals – a young woman and her little children – so, you should have no problem getting the better of someone you called a pipsqueak. Come on! Let's see how brave you *really* are!'

'You dare to challenge *me*?' Zorn thundered, and repeated his assault, but with the same embarrassing lack of success.

Young Mungo laughed out loud, while the Keelie mob jostled for position to watch the long-awaited showdown that was finally kicking off in earnest.

Meanwhile, Susie and Jamie stood huddled together behind Mungo, desperately waiting their chance to run to their mother's side. Then something within the still-descending cage caught Jamie's eye: in their scramble to make good their own escape, they had left their two pets behind. Without a second's hesitation, Jamie started to squeeze back through the hole in the side of the cage. By the time Susie noticed, it was too late to stop him, although she suspected it would have been pointless to even try. The bond that existed between Jamie, his mouse *and* their dog would not be broken. And, knowing him, the possibility of being burned alive with them would already have been banished from his mind.

Zorn's attack on Mungo was becoming increasingly frenzied, yet even the two-handed bolts of lightning he now hurled were being instantly vaporised by the magic staff. Mungo was duly emboldened, and took further encouragement from seeing trickles of perspiration beginning to glisten on Zorn's brow. But he knew that, no matter how futile Zorn's current efforts might appear, he was still capable of inflicting lethal damage. Consequently, Mungo was concentrating hard on defending himself; so hard, in fact, that he was totally oblivious to what was happening behind his back...

Jamie was now inside the cage, the escape hole growing smaller with every click of the chain, the inferno below roaring ever closer. He snatched Jasper from his tiny prison and put him in his pocket, then reached up and freed Charlie from his cage. Susie, trying her best to hold her nerve, dropped trembling to her knees on the floor of the dais, her hands outstretched, waiting for Jamie to hand her their little dog.

As for Zorn, he was too caught up in his life-or-death confrontation with Mungo to take any notice of the children. He was already looking less cocksure of himself than usual, his face dripping sweat, his chest heaving. He took a faltering step forward, steadied himself and adopted his spell-casting stance, legs apart, one hand pointing at Mungo. 'The time for playing games is over!' he muttered, then took a slow, deep breath and growled. '*ABLAN, ABLAN – INIMICO NECARABBO!*'

Young Mungo was instantly enshrouded in snaking ribbons of electrical energy, which buzzed and spat as they writhed over him. On the wall, the image of the Devil's face twisted into a fiendish smile, and on the cavern floor, the Keelie crowds yelled in delight.

But with a flick of his staff, Mungo cast the deadly shroud from his body, then gave a devil-may-care laugh. 'You'll have to do better than that, Zorn! After all, when was a lion ever troubled by a flea?'

Zorn was incensed. How dare this upstart treat his proven superior with such disrespect! The Devil's disciple, a *flea*? Oh, but he would make Mungo pay dearly for that!

Inside the cage, Jamie was on his tiptoes, holding Charlie aloft, struggling to push him through what little of the opening remained above the rim of the pit. But just as he succeeded in delivering the little dog into the safety of his sister's hands, the cage took another downwards jolt, completely shutting off his only way out.

So shrill were Susie's screams that they cut through the cacophony of noises already reverberating throughout the cavern. Mungo turned automatically towards her cries. Assessing the situation in a flash, he realised that the first thing he had to do was halt the descent of the cage. He looked up and pointed his staff at the cog wheels through which the supporting chain was looped.

And this was the chance Zorn had been waiting for. He directed a lightning bolt at Mungo's back, knocking him into the gap between the cage and the wall of the pit. As he fell, Mungo managed to grasp a bar of the cage, but in so doing let go of the staff. Without access to its Power, there was no longer anything he could do to stop the cage continuing its click-by-click descent into the raging inferno.

Zorn was now standing at the edge of the pit, staring down at Mungo dangling from the cage, with little Jamie cowering inside. One of Zorn's Keelie flunkies shuffled forward, lifted the sacred staff from the floor and handed it to his master. The tables had now turned, and the look on Zorn's face made it abundantly clear that he intended to take full advantage.

'So, Mungo,' he smirked, 'history repeats itself. For without this twig, you are nothing – finished!' He gripped the ends of the staff and lifted it above his head. 'And this time, I will not only break it in two, but will make certain that all that remains of it are ashes!'

But as he prepared to bring the staff down on his knee, he yowled in agony. Charlie the dog had leapt from Susie's arms, had sunk his teeth into Zorn's ankle, and was worrying it as if it were a rat. Shouting curses, Zorn hopped about on one foot, trying to shake Charlie off. In his fluster, he let go of the staff, which clattered to the floor and came to rest with one end jutting over the edge of the pit.

This did not go unnoticed by Mungo, but even at full stretch he couldn't quite get a hand to it. Then he became aware of Susie peering apprehensively into the pit. 'Quick!' he shouted up to her. 'The staff! Hand me down the staff!'

Though terrified, Susie edged her way round the perimeter of the hole, carefully avoiding Zorn, who was frantically attempting to set Charlie up for a lightning strike. 'When I get you off,' he growled, 'I'll scorch you to a frazzle, you mangy cur!'

But the little dog had his teeth firmly embedded in his ankle and wasn't about to let go.

A group of Keelies had gathered round, crouched and ready to snatch Charlie away from their master's leg. And so intently were they following the action that they hadn't immediately noticed Susie picking up the staff. But before she could pass it down to Mungo, she was seized by one sharp-eyed Keelie, then another, and another. In the ensuing struggle, the staff was wrenched away from her and flung into the pit.

Mungo clutched at it as it tumbled past the cage, but it slipped through his fingers, leaving him to watch in despair as it rattled down against the wall of the pit towards the boiling cauldron of flames. It seemed that the forces of good really had deserted him this time, and in the harshest of ways. Yet, no sooner had he thought all wast lost than he was handed a lifeline, albeit a slender one. The staff landed and became precariously balanced on a small ledge, where it rocked back and forth, poised to continue its fall at the first touch of the descending cage.

Young Mungo peered up through the mouth of the pit to where the supporting chain entered the cog wheels, and was horrified to see that only a few more links remained to be drawn through. There wasn't a moment to spare.

'The staff, boy!' he shouted to Jamie. 'Try to take hold of it – it's our only hope!'

Jamie crept gingerly over the floor of the cage and stretched one hand as far as he could through the bars, his fingers feeling blindly into the smoke.

Zorn, meanwhile, finally succeeded in dislodging Charlie from his ankle. The little dog wasted no time in making a dash for it, ducking and diving between the legs and grasping hands of the Keelies. Zorn was quick to fire the promised lightning bolt, which only just missed Charlie as he nipped round a corner and out of sight. One of the Keelies was about to give chase, but Zorn would have none of it.

'Later!' he snapped. 'The stupid mutt cannot get out of here.' He indicated Susie with a sideways nod of his head. 'The brat first. Take her to her mother! '

The Keelie mob on the floor howled their approval, and those on the dais milled round Zorn as he strutted to the altar. Susie was pushed, struggling and squealing, to stand in front of him. With the image of the Devil grinning down from the wall, one of the Keelies grabbed Susie's hair, pulled her head back and forced her to look at Zorn's face.

He stared into her eyes, his own radiating a mesmerising green glow. *'Ablan dormabbo,'* he droned. *'Dormabbo … dormabbo … dormabbo.'*

All the fight drained from Susie, and she swooned against her captors in a trance. Zorn motioned the Keelies to lift her onto the altar beside her mother. The doleful thrum of organ chords and the wailing of the phantom choir began to swell again as one of Zorn's sidekicks stepped forward and presented him with the dagger Mungo had blasted from his hand earlier.

Zorn eyed it with malignant relish, then roared, 'NOW, LET THE SACRIFICE PROCEED!'

Young Mungo made a frantic effort to haul himself out of the pit. But the more he struggled to find a handhold on the bars of the cage, the more it swung on its chain, thumping his back against the rough stone. He glanced upwards again, and saw that the end of the chain had now disappeared into the system of cog wheels. In a matter of seconds, the cage would plunge unchecked into the waiting inferno. Everything now depended on Jamie.

In the interim, Susie had been laid on the altar beside her mother. Zorn loomed over them, cradling the sacrificial dagger in his hands, then wheeled round to face the Devil.

'*In the name of all that is evil*,' he proclaimed, '*I present you, oh omnipotent Lucifer, with this humble offering!*'

Thunder rolled and the Keelie crowds howled in acclamation as the Devil indicated his assent with a slow nodding of his head. Zorn now turned back to face the altar, raising the knife above his head, the hilt held in both hands, the blade pointing down towards his two unconscious victims.

Inside the cage, Jamie at last managed to stretch his arm far enough through the bars to make contact with the staff, but the merest touch of his finger tips was all it took to make it swivel tantalisingly out of reach again. Spurred on by Mungo, he swiped at it feverishly until it began to see-saw on the brink of the ledge, presenting Mungo with his last chance to deliver them from this sweltering death trap. Mungo clung to the outside of cage with one hand, while straining every muscle to snatch the end of the staff the moment it pivoted upwards. And his timing could not have been better. His fingers closed round the staff just as it was about to topple off the ledge, and only a heartbeat before the last link in the cage's supporting chain clicked into the cogs. With a slash of the staff, Mungo cut Jamie free from the cage, then magicked them both out of the pit with a snappy '*ZIBANNO*!'

Back on the dais, Zorn was completing his dedication to the Devil. He threw his head back and, staring up at the sacrificial dagger, shouted, '*So, with this instrument of death, I commit these mortal souls to* –'

'You, Zorn, are unable to commit them to *any*thing!' a voice rang out.

Zorn caught his breath, and looked over his shoulder to see Young Mungo standing there, the ancient staff held out in front of him, little Jamie at his side, clinging to his robe.

'Curse you to purgatory!' Zorn barked. 'I will deal with you and your pathetic twig in a moment – once and for all!

A shrug of indifference was Mungo's response.

Zorn turned his back and raised the sacrificial knife once more. 'I have dedicated the souls of these mortals to Satan, and to Satan they will go. *NOW!*' With that, he brought the knife down with all his might. But before it could pierce Maggie's chest, Zorn was sent staggering by a dazzling burst of energy from the tip of Mungo's staff. The knife flew from his hand and became lodged, hilt-first, in a cleft of the wall immediately below the scowling face of Satan.

Stunned, Zorn steadied himself, then, in a voice trembling with fury, yelled at the Keelie mob, 'Seize him! Seize the usurper Mungo, the pathetic weakling who dares to assault your lord and master with his ludicrous magic wand. Seize him, and hurl him back into the pit!'

Every Keelie knew well enough the Power of the ancient staff, so none would have been so foolhardy as to tackle Mungo single-handedly. But there were may of them, and as if by instinct, they spread out and advanced on him from three sides. Mungo watched them intently, pointing the staff in a wide arc. But he couldn't cover them all. He was also acutely aware that Zorn was lurking over by the altar, and although in a weakened state, would be ready to take advantage of any attack the Keelies might launch. Mungo was on the back foot, with the mouth of the fiery pit only a couple of steps behind him.

One of the Keelies fired a lightning bolt, which Mungo parried with the staff. A second Keelie did

likewise from another position on the floor. More
Keelies followed suit, all from different angles.
Mungo deflected each strike in turn, but this was
getting tricky.

Jamie tugged at his robe. 'Too many bad goblins,
mister! Better magic us out of here quick. Oh, and
don't forget Charlie – *or* Mummy and Susie!'

Mungo glanced over to the altar, where Maggie
and her daughter lay exposed to whatever act of
brutality Zorn now chose to inflict on them. Jamie's
suggestion to magic them all out of there was well
intended, but easier said than done. Nevertheless,
the little fellow's observation about bad goblins *did*
give Mungo an idea. He raised his eyes heavenward,
made a hurried appeal to the Mighty One, then said
under his breath, '*Kiltiae ad expedanno*!'

Through the clamour of conflict now raging
within the cavern, there emerged the faint skirl of
bagpipes. Mungo smiled down at Jamie and patted
his head. 'Thank you, young man. If you hadn't
mentioned bad goblins, I'd never have thought of –'

'I told you, the time for playing games is over,'
Zorn barked, and bombarded Mungo with shafts of
fire from his eyes.

Mungo again used his staff as a shield. But this left
him unprotected from the attentions of the Keelies,
who grabbed the chance to redouble their onslaught
and drive their two victims back to the very brink
of the pit.

Jamie ventured a peek into the fiery chasm, and
felt a wave of panic rising with the heat. 'Phew!
Better bring back the blackbird quick, mister! We

need more magic pennies!'

But even if his suggestion had offered some chance of deliverance, it would still have gone unheeded by Mungo, whose concentration had become totally focused on dealing with Zorn. It was now a matter of which of the warring wizards would yield first.

For want of anywhere better to take shelter, Jamie got down on all fours and crept under the hem of Mungo's robe, which drew howls of laughter from the Keelies as they advanced en masse. In the vanguard were Scurvo and Tentor, the most fawning of Zorn's flunkies, who had sneaked out from wherever they'd been hiding while there was any risk of their being caught in the crossfire. *Their* target, as might be expected, was not Mungo, but young Jamie. To his credit, the little fellow clung to Mungo's ankles like a koala on a gum tree and kicked out with both feet, but there was never any doubt that his resistance to these brawny little devils would be short-lived.

Although Mungo could not risk taking his eyes off Zorn for one second, he knew the cause of the turmoil erupting within the nether regions of his robe could only be attributed to one thing. 'Hold on, Master Jamie,' he urged. 'Believe in the good and deny the bad!' Then he filled his lungs and bellowed, '*KILTIAE … KILTIAE ZIBANNO-O-O-OH*!'

Not a moment too soon, the strident sound of bagpipes rose in volume to compete with the prevailing din within the cavern, and from the shadows of a tunnel at the far side there emerged a massed pipe band of goblins. Dressed in full Highland costume of tartan kilts, swinging sporrans, billowing plaids and Balmoral bonnets with ribbons fluttering, they were playing a stirring march. They fanned out, as if making their entrance onto the castle esplanade for the finale of the Edinburgh Military Tattoo. Leading them was a swaggering drum major, brandishing his mace in grand style, while behind the ranks of pipers came the goblin drum corps, snare drummers rattling a sprightly rhythm, bass drummers thumping out the beat.

Scurvo and Tentor knew trouble when they saw it, so promptly made themselves scarce again, leaving Jamie to peep unhindered from under Mungo's robe.

'The Kilties!' he gasped, his face wreathed in smiles. 'Still plenty goodie goblins about, just like old Mungo said!'

If *young* Mungo had been able to hear Jamie's final comment amid the ongoing hubbub, he may well have allowed himself a wry smile.

In any event, the Keelies on the cavern floor were *certainly* smiling, laughing in fact, but for a very different reason. They had turned to face the advancing Kilties, shouting insults, making rude gestures and trying to impress one another with sarcastic remarks.

Still playing, the Kilties formed up line-abreast in front of them and proceeded to march on the spot.

Much to the amusement of his comrades, one of the Keelies started to mimic the pipers, pumping his left elbow up and down, puffing out his cheeks like an amorous bullfrog, holding his nose and making noises akin to the wheezing of a clapped-out vacuum cleaner.

Without missing a beat, the Kiltie drum major threw his mace in the air, deftly caught it again and used it as a rocket launcher to zap the cocky Keelie, who dissolved into a wispy green smoke ring after being propelled head-over-heels with sparks flying from his nostrils and steam belching from his ears.

This served as a signal for the Kiltie pipers to stop playing and go down on one knee, aiming their bagpipes rifle-style at the Keelie mob. The Kiltie drummers duly positioned themselves in battle formation behind the pipers, casually twirling their drumsticks between their fingers. They were chewing gum and wearing shades, the way drummers do. If these Keelie grease bags were looking for a scrap – cool – bring it on!

And it didn't take long for the Kilties to get to grips with their scourge-of-the-goblin-world foes. Although the Keelies blitzed them from all angles with wave after wave of lightning bolts, the Kiltie drummers intercepted them by launching their drum sticks as whirling chopper blades, which minced the missiles into nothing more threatening than showers of twinkling fairy lights. The pipers in turn pounded the Keelie lines with laser beams blazing from their bagpipes. It was a well-drilled and spectacularly effective military exercise, which resulted in seven bells being knocked out of the entire Keelie pack before they fully realised what was hitting them. The Kilties were the ones laughing now, marching off in triumph after making short work of blasting their enemies into an aerial ballet of evaporating smoke rings.

On the dais, Mungo was still using the staff to deflect the death rays shooting out from Zorn's eyes, but had started to move forward, one cautious step at a time. For Zorn was tiring, his supernatural abilities waning, his legs becoming weak, his breathing laboured.

'Damn you, Mungo!' he snarled as the shafts of fire from his eyes began to fade and falter against the impregnable Power of the staff. He staggered back towards the wall from which the Devil's image continued to look down, though notably less domineeringly than before.

Jamie had been shuffling along in Mungo's wake, daring only to snatch an occasional glance at the terrifying goings-on from behind the sanctuary of his robe. But all the while, the little boy's main concern had had little to do with flame-throwing contests between all these freaky characters. So, he jumped at the chance afforded by this temporary lull in proceedings to slip past Mungo and run to the altar, where he stared distraught at his mother and sister, lying motionless side-by-side.

'Mummy,' he sobbed. 'Susie. Wake up! Wake *up*! Don't be dead! Don't leave me ... *please*!'

But neither as much as flickered an eyelid.

Gesturing towards this heart-rending scene, young Mungo glared at Zorn. 'You must be really proud of what you have done in the name of your vile master!'

But Zorn was blatantly unrepentant. 'You dare speak ill of *him*?'

'There are no words foul enough to describe him,

or anyone who subscribes to his contemptible creed.'

Zorn pointed up to the image of the Devil, then glowered at Mungo with hatred in his eyes. 'I call upon the invincible force of *his* will to destroy you and all you stand for!'

'And in the name of all that is good,' Mungo countered, 'I invite him to do his worst!'

There followed some moments of palpable tension as Zorn worked himself into a fever of loathing. *'Per novem malevo,'* he eventually snarled, his voice breaking, *'Per novem malevo – MORIABBO!'*

As thunder rolled, a searing beam of light shot down from the Devil's eyes, enveloping Mungo and setting the floor around his feet on fire. Assuming an air of indifference, Mungo stood smiling and shaking his head at Zorn, who began to laugh manically while screaming entreaties to the Devil. It was obvious to Mungo that Zorn was really feeling the pressure now, dependent as he was on the Devil's help in overcoming the threat of all things good that the staff represented. With studied calm, Mungo faced the Devil, held the sacred rod vertically in front of his chest and extended his forearm over it to form the shape of a cross.

A ghastly howl echoed through the cavern as the Devil's face twisted in agony, while the beam enveloping Mungo guttered and died, like the flame of a candle buffeted by a sudden gust of wind.

Zorn, now in a visible state of panic, pleaded with the Devil to strike Mungo down. But the image of the Devil's face had already started to fall apart, its features melting into a shapeless mess and dribbling down the wall in ripples of red slime. Mungo stepped slowly but deliberately towards Zorn, who backed away, a hand raised to shield his eyes from the glow of the cross.

'Damn you, Mungo!' he called out again, his voice a quivering apology for the fearsome growl that had struck terror into so many poor wretches through the ages. Squinting at Mungo like a dazzled rabbit, he tottered backwards, stumbled, and slammed his back against the wall. Hard. A look of shocked disbelief contorted his face as his eyes were drawn to a gory stain spreading from where the point of the sacrificial dagger was protruding from his chest.

Mungo's expression was a mix of revulsion and pity as he recalled the words Zorn had spoken when about to stab Maggie to death: *'With this blade, forged in the flames of hell, and from whose thrust no living body can survive...'* He paused to reach out and touch the top of Zorn's head, before murmuring, 'May your tormented soul find peace.'

Zorn was in his death throes, struggling for breath, choking, green blood trickling from his mouth. But still he found the strength to look up and splutter, 'The power of evil is – is indestructible. And I – I swear, Mungo, one day … one day…'

As Zorn breathed his last, his head rolled to one side and he slumped impaled against the wall. Mungo looked on while the body of this once-respected and highly-gifted wizard, who had chosen to devote his life to bringing about the Devil's domination of the mortal world, crumbled into an insignificant heap of dust, to be blown away on a gentle breeze now wafting through the cavern.

With the breeze came a bright, shining light, spreading into the shadows to replace with a feeling of goodwill the dark mood of despair that had been the hallmark of Zorn's underworld domain. And a soothing calm settled all around, bringing total silence, save for the whisper of the breeze.

Mungo looked up towards the source of the light, and there appeared within it the face of The Master, his beloved mentor when but a callow student of wizardry all those centuries ago. Though at death's door himself, the old Grand Sorcerer's final act before ascending to the Higher Place had been to save Mungo from being slain by Zorn, following his brutal devastation of Goblin Hall Castle and desecration of the sacred staff. And Mungo knew full well that, without The Master's intervention, his survival against Zorn today would not have been possible either.

He was about to offer up his thanks, but The Master held a silencing finger to his lips. 'As I advised you on that fateful day long, long ago, when first I recognised your potential as a sorcerer of rare ability, there is no harm in hoping for the best, but never take it for granted.' He gave an impish wink. 'A maxim, I believe, a certain levitated piglet would endorse.' His expression grew more serious as he added, 'And never forget, although good has triumphed over bad on this occasion, there will always be Zorns of some sort or other, who will emerge at unforeseen times to undermine the foundations of what is right and decent.' He smiled kindly and raised his hand.

'Now, go forth into the light, my son. For look, your little family of mortals awaits you...'

On the altar, which was now draped in pristine white, Maggie and Susie were beginning to stir – blinking their eyes and yawning, as if waking from a deep sleep.

Jamie clambered up beside them, grinning from ear to ear. He hugged his mother as she and Susie sat up, looking around in bewilderment.

'Mummy! Jamie!' Susie chirped after a moment or two. 'We – we're together again! *Really* together again!'

With tears of joy in her eyes, Maggie pulled the children to her. 'Oh, Susie, Jamie ... I've found you at last, and I promise I'll never lose you again. Never, never, *never*!'

Young Mungo slowly approached the altar, where he stopped and looked down at this blissful reunion of a mother and her children, a truly wonderful occasion that had come perilously close to never happening.

When Maggie noticed him, her heart skipped a beat. 'It can't be,' she whispered, then closed her eyes and opened them again, hesitantly. A startled but joyful look lit her face, but was quickly dimmed by a frown of suspicion. 'It can't be,' she said again. '*Can* it?'

Confused and somewhat concerned by their mother's mixed emotions, Susie and Jamie followed her stare. Their mouths fell open, the looks on *their* faces also suggesting disbelief at what they were seeing. Then, very gradually, tentative little smiles grew into grins of cautious optimism, until, with all doubts finally banished, they jumped up, clapping their hands together in an outburst of unbridled delight.

'It *is*!' squealed Susie.

'It's *him*!' squealed Jamie.

'It's *DADDY*!' they squealed together.

Maggie was in such a delirium of happiness that she didn't know whether to laugh or cry. 'Jim?' she whispered through her tears. 'You – you've come back to us! But how – how can that be?'

His only reply was a reassuring smile, which was all that Maggie and the children needed. He was there, and nothing else mattered any more.

Then Charlie the dog appeared from only-he-knew-where, leapt onto the altar and wasted no time in contributing to the spirit of celebration by licking everyone's face.

And this was Jamie's cue to pull his pet white mouse from his pocket and hold him up by the tail. 'There you are, Jasper,' he chuckled, 'I promised I'd save you, didn't I?'

Maggie rolled her eyes. 'And thereby *really* hangs a tale!'

They all had a good laugh at that, then Maggie and the children huddled together and nuzzled their heads against Jim's chest.

'Come on,' he said, folding his arms around them, 'I think it's time we all went home now, don't you?'

* * * * *

– EPILOGUE –

TROWIE GLEN – THE PRESENT DAY...

Maggie and Jim were trudging up the hill towards the old dead tree, carrying a large picnic basket between them and enjoying the summer sunshine. Susie and Jamie were scampering around, giggling and shouting and playing chase with Charlie the dog.

'Jim?' said Maggie, in a tentative sort of way.

'Uh-huh.'

'Do, uhm, do you believe in … magic?'

'Well, you know,' Jim replied matter-of-factly, 'I'm a minister, so, magic, miracles, much the same, some would say.'

Susie and Jamie exchanged where-have-we-heard-that-before? glances, and they knew it wasn't from their father.

'Hmm, maybe so, Jim,' Maggie went on, 'but I was – well, I was thinking more of wizards, that kind of magic.'

'*Wizards*?'

'That's right. You know, people with supernatural powers – people who can live for centuries, change their identity and perform all sorts of unbelievable feats, some good, some bad.'

Jim gave a little laugh. 'I think "unbelievable" sums up the whole idea. Anyway, what brings all this on?'

'Oh, nothing really. Just that I had this strange dream last night.'

They had reached the top of the hill, so Jim bent down to spread the rug he had been carrying. 'A strange dream? What kind of strange?'

Maggie began emptying the picnic things from the hamper. 'Not just strange, but creepy too. And absolutely frightening at times.'

'Sounds like a bit of a nightmare, if you ask me.'

'Nightmare isn't the word for it. And it was all so real. Yes, and sad as well.'

'Sad? How do you mean?'

Maggie wasn't sure how to answer that in front of the children, who had already seated themselves on the edge of the rug and were keenly awaiting any interesting information that might be forthcoming on the subject of wizards. So, rather than tell Jim bluntly that he had been dead for most of the dream, she said, 'Well, let's just say that you had gone *missing* for a while and – well, so had the kids and, to find them, I had to trust in this young wizard...' Maggie paused and fired a disapproving glance at Jamie, who had pulled something from his pocket and was placing it carefully down in front of him. 'I *told* you not to bring that white mouse, Jamie!'

'But, Mum, you don't understand,' Susie piped up in defence of her little brother, 'it's Jasper and –'

'I don't care what his name is. He can't sniff about

on the rug like that. It's not hygienic. So, Jamie, put him in there until we've finished eating!' She opened the empty hamper, then muttered tetchily, 'I've had enough trouble over a white mouse in dreamland, without having the picnic spoiled by one as well!'

'Anyway,' Jim said, 'you were telling me about some young wizard or other.'

'Yes, Mungo was his name, and he was actually ancient before he got young.'

'Ancient *before* he got young?' Jim seemed to be trying hard not to laugh.

But Maggie wasn't kidding. 'And – and he was kind of dotty. Well, pretty useless, actually.'

'Useless?'

'Yes, *completely* useless at times – and he turned out to be you.'

'Me?'

'That's right, but before he was you, he was going to be bumped off by this wicked wizard and his mob of evil goblins, somewhere deep under the ruins of the old castle down there. That was until he summoned up some special kind of mystical power he'd got from being struck by lightning under this old dead tree here.'

Jim looked up at the tracery of naked branches. 'Struck by lightning? Here? And survived?'

Susie and Jamie were sitting enthralled, all ears and taking every word seriously.

'It's true though, Dad,' said Susie. 'And we've got a book that proves it!'

'Yes,' Jamie chipped in. '*Wizard of the Hen*'.

'It's *Glen*, silly!' Susie frowned. 'I keep telling

you that!'

'Ah,' Jim nodded, 'that explains it, Maggie. I seem to remember reading that book to the kids once. You probably have as well, and all the wizard stuff has stuck at the back of your mind and popped up in your dream.'

Maggie wasn't convinced. 'Maybe, but I've never had a dream as real as that before. I mean, it was as if we were all really *there*.'

'That happens with dreams sometimes. It happens to all of us,' Jim assured her, 'so don't worry about it.'

While everyone was gabbling about dreams and wizards, Charlie the dog snatched a chipolata sausage from Maggie's plate and slunk behind the children to enjoy it in peace.

'I *know* dreams can seem real occasionally,' Maggie agreed, 'but this was different somehow. I mean, I've just remembered, when the wizard Mungo – that's the young Mungo, after he was old – was trying to hypnotise me to stop me from being so persistent when I was trying to save the children from these slimy dragon-type monsters, I noticed something familiar about his eyes.' Maggie leaned forward and peered into Jim's face. 'I couldn't put my finger on it at the time, but I see it now. Mungo's eyes were yours. Yet the rest of him wasn't you … until later.'

Sighing, Jim poured Maggie a coffee from the thermos. 'Goblins, slimy dragons, an ancient wizard who becomes young and turns into me. OK, some would say that's all unreal enough, but to suggest that you could be *persistent*, Maggie – well, that really *is* beyond belief!' Jim gave Maggie a playful wink. He also crossed his fingers behind his back.

Maggie didn't notice this, but the children did.

'What does that sign mean?' Jamie whispered to Susie.

'Not sure, but I think grown-up people do it when they've told a fib.'

They both thought about that for a while.

'Maybe it means Daddy really *is* a wizard,' Jamie suggested at length.

Susie tapped her top lip, still thinking. 'Could be – sort of. Mmm, and he did say the same as old Mungo said about magic and miracles being the same. Anyway, little brother, don't ask him to make Jasper fly, whatever you do!'

'Won't even ask him to make nose pennies appear again,' Jamie mumbled, frowning now too. He shook his head, vigorously. 'Not ever, ever, *ever*!'

'Good idea,' Susie concurred in her big-sisterly way. 'Yes, Jamie,' she stressed, while reaching out to grab a jam doughnut, 'best to leave these things to real wizards from now on.'

Jamie nodded his agreement, smiled a satisfied smile, then helped himself to a fairy cake.

'Because,' Susie added as an afterthought, 'we have to believe in the good and deny the bad.'

'Just like old Mungo said as well,' said Jamie, and proceeded to stuff a whole fairy cake into his mouth.

'Absolutely right,' Susie affirmed through a hail of doughnut crumbs. ''Cause although we can't deny that Daddy is *not* a bad man, I really don't believe he'd make a very good wizard either.'

'Assalooty right,' said Jamie, whose thoughts had already drifted to less complex, more pressing issues. 'Uhm, pass the sammidges, please!' he shouted across the rug to his mother. 'But not the coo-cumbo ones. They make me sick!'

* * *

Outside a little cottage at the foot of the glen, meanwhile, an old man was sitting on his rocking chair, a look of deep contentment on his face.

'And so, my little feathered friend,' he said to the young jackdaw perched on his shoulder, 'as my story has illustrated, not *every*thing is always as it seems.'

'*Algabooraba*,' croaked the jackdaw.

'Clever boy!' grinned the old man, and gave the bird a titbit.

With a rasping cry of '*ZIBANNO*!' the jackdaw fluttered onto the cottage roof, but only after plopping a dropping down the old man's back.

For the moment at least, the old man was unaware of what he would surely have regarded as the jackdaw's regrettable lack of decorum. His attention was drawn instead to a gold coin the bird had deposited on his lap, and he gave a little chuckle as a flicker of lightning shimmered in the distance and a murmur of thunder rumbled round the hills.

'A very clever boy indeed,' he said to himself, holding the coin aloft to allow its glow to meld with the gilded tops of turrets rising majestically through woods on the other side of the glen. 'Hmm,' he mused, while marvelling at the elegance of a winged piglet looping and swooping in a cloudless sky above the castle, 'but *any*thing is possible … if you believe.'

* * *

THE END

ALSO BY PETER KERR:

'SNOWBALL ORANGES'
- One Mallorcan Winter -

First in the bestselling series of five books charting the Kerr family's often hilarious adventures after leaving Scotland to grow oranges for a living on the Spanish island of Mallorca.

"Immensely engaging and amusing."

"Full of life and colour – a haven of Mediterranean sunshine."

"The story is carried effortlessly through on an entertaining raft of humour."

(Paperback ISBN 978-1-78685-042-3)

Full details of this and all Peter's other titles are on his website: **www.peter-kerr.co.uk**

Printed in Great Britain
by Amazon